Killer Drop

Mette Bach

James Lorimer & Company Ltd., Publishers
Toronto

Copyright © by Mette Bach
Canadian edition published in 2016. United States edition published in 2017.

James Lorimer & Company Ltd., Publishers acknowledges the support of the Ontario Arts Council. We acknowledge the support of the Canada Council for the Arts which last year invested $24.3 million in writing and publishing throughout Canada. We acknowledge the Government of Ontario through the Ontario Media Development Corporation's Ontario Book Initiative.

ONTARIO ARTS COUNCIL
CONSEIL DES ARTS DE L'ONTARIO

The Canada Council | Le Conseil des Arts
for the Arts | du Canada

Canadä

Cover design: Tyler Cleroux
Cover image: Shutterstock

Library and Archives Canada Cataloguing in Publication

Bach, Mette, 1976-, author
    Killer drop / Mette Bach.

(SideStreets)
Issued in print and electronic formats.
ISBN 978-1-4594-1090-9 (paperback).--ISBN 978-1-4594-1091-6 (epub)

    I. Title. II. Series: SideStreets

PS8603.A298K54 2016   jC813'.6   C2015-907213-1
                                                     C2015-907214-X

James Lorimer & Company Ltd., Publishers 317 Adelaide Street West, Suite 1002 Toronto, ON, Canada M5V 1P9 www.lorimer.ca	Canadian edition (978-1-4594-1090-9) distributed by: Formac Lorimer Books 5502 Atlantic Street Halifax, NS, Canada B3H 1G4	American edition (978-1-4594-1093-0.) distributed by: Lerner Publishing Group 1251 Washington Ave N Minneapolis, MN, USA 55401

Printed and bound in Canada.
Manufactured by Friesens Corporation in Altona, Manitoba, Canada in January 2016.
Job #220111

For Seals and Nerdog

Prologue

It was my first day at Montrose Academy. I was going into grade nine and taking a selfie with Mom and Dad outside Oakley Hall, the biggest building on the school grounds. It's where everyone does their photo since it has that Oxford look with the ivy-covered old bricks. My family has gone here for generations. We have a picture at home of my grandfather dropping my dad off on his first day in front of the very same building.

"Don't forget, Marcus," Dad said. "If anyone gives you a hard time, you look at their library books and tell them you own that library. Your grandfather paid for that whole wing, so don't let anyone push you around."

I'd never been pushed around before, and I wasn't about to start. But it was kind of fun to think about. If anyone pulled the kind of high school stunts you see in movies, I could tell them to eff off and remind them that my family could buy their family and eat them for breakfast. Not bad.

Once the photo was done, I headed in. My old friends from last year were all there in their fresh new uniforms, black shirts with white collars. They were embossed with the Montrose Magpies crest, like Lacoste shirts but with birds instead of alligators. I joined them.

"Can't wait to see who this year's peasant will be," Ozzie said.

"Huh?"

"You know. The scholarship student. I hear

he's not even from West Van this time, just moved here to go to school."

Then we saw him: a scrawny, Chinese nerd with a peach-and-white striped T-shirt. The shirt was a mistake.

"He's like a little earthworm," Kayla said, looking at Ozzie, clearly trying to make him laugh. He grinned.

We watched a guidance counsellor hand him a uniform. He went into the boys' room and came out looking like us, but not. Maybe it was that he didn't pay for the uniform on his parents' unlimited credit. Something about him screamed "charity case."

"Oh my God," Kayla said. "He still looks like a worm."

"How'd you wriggle in here?" Ozzie said to him when he walked by us.

I laughed because Ozzie's such a blow horn. That guy has never been able to hold back. But the new guy stopped in his tracks and looked Ozzie straight in the face.

"Through the front door just like you," he said, then walked past us down the corridor. This simple statement totally baffled Ozzie, who stood there with his mouth wide open. I guess he wasn't expecting the guy to answer him.

Kayla watched him go, and when he was almost out of earshot, she yelled, "Worm!"

He didn't turn around. Everyone laughed, including me. It was the shirt. Terrible choice. And the uniform didn't change a thing.

Kayla went, "No, but seriously, am I right? He still totally looks like one."

There were smiles and nods all over the place. But soon they went back to talking about what they did over the summer: Hawaii, Italy and Paris. Sailing, golfing and horseback riding. I got a sinking feeling that real high school was not that different from the way it looks in horrible American movies.

One day, a few months into grade nine, the weirdest thing happened. We were in

English, and I was copying Worm's answers (it's good to have peasants around for things like that) when out of nowhere, he asked me if I've ever been fishing. I kind of laughed. Who goes fishing anymore? But he told me his dad was taking him for the weekend and asked if I wanted to go. "Sure," I said. "Why not?"

That weekend changed everything. Worm became my best friend, only I started calling him Tom instead. Over the next couple of years, we spent most of our weekends together. His dad, Ed, took us camping and got us to help out whenever he did repairs around their house. A couple of summers ago, we even built a garage.

Tom lives in this cramped little hovel that his grandparents bought in the fifties or something, long before West Van got snooty. The whole family's been cooped up in this tiny shack just so Tom could go to Montrose. It's shitty and awesome all at the same time. So usually we'd go there to eat because his grandma, his Poh Poh, is always in the kitchen making something delicious. Then we'd go to my place to play video games and spread out. Between our two places and my Jeep, by grade twelve, we pretty much had it made.

Chapter 1

Fringe Benefits

After school, Tom meets me at my locker. We leave school and get into my blue Jeep. I drive us to the Mountain Equipment Co-op where he works, down by the Canadian Tire on Brooksbank off Cotton Road. His boss said we could try out some new ski gear and write it up in the catalogue and on the website, so the plan is to grab the goggles, jackets, boots and bindings and head up one of the local mountains just to do a few runs on our boards.

Well, *I'll* use *my* board. Tom can use my sister Steph's. She doesn't mind.

"I dunno," Tom says as we pull into the parking lot. "I should probably just go home and study tonight."

"Dude, you're the one who set this up."

"I failed my Econ assignment. I have to make up for it on the test."

"*You?* Fail?"

"Asian fail," he corrects, laughing. "I got a B."

"Come on, Worm. One run isn't going to kill you. We'll be back by six, latest."

Tom hates when I call him Worm, the way everyone else does, but it's my secret weapon. He'll go along with anything when I do it.

"Easy for you to say." Tom raises his hand and squeezes his thumb and forefinger together like he's about to crush an insect. "I'm this close to losing my scholarship, and if that happens, my chances of getting an entrance scholarship to a good university are over."

"Quit being a drama queen," I tell him. "There're only five months of high school left. What could possibly go wrong?"

"You're right, you're right." He undoes his seatbelt and hops out of the Jeep. "Let's go for a killer run."

We go into the store. Tom's boss sets us up with supplier samples and tells us what he expects us to notice about the gear and comment on in our reports. Then off we go.

Cypress, Grouse and Seymour are impressive mountains if you're from the prairies, but I grew up skiing and boarding at Whistler, so for me, these so-called mountains are really just foothills. But whatever. I turn up Lillooet Road to Seymour. It's definitely cool that Tom's boss wants us to write reviews and maybe even model the stuff for the website. It almost makes me want to get a job just so I can do cool stuff like this, but I hate having to show up places on time.

We whoosh down the slopes a few times,

and then pack it in for the night.

"Pretty good jacket," I comment. "Warm. Lightweight. Good for backcountry."

"Not bad," Tom agrees. "But I wouldn't pay retail for it."

"You wouldn't pay retail for anything."

By the time we get back to the store, I've decided to get a couple of the jackets in different colours. I need a new one for the ski trip coming up anyway, and I go up to Whistler at least a dozen times every winter, and there is nothing worse than being wet on the slopes.

Before checking out, I pick up some new thermal socks, a wool sweater and some better-fitting ski pants. I grab the jacket Tom was wearing — it's obvious he likes it — and slap my platinum card on the counter.

In the car, Tom says, "Dude, you just spent a couple grand in there. You should have at least let me get you my staff discount."

"*Pfft*," I say. "Whatevs, man."

He rolls his eyes. "I can get my own jacket, you know. I'm not that much of a peasant. Besides, I have a job."

"Don't worry about it. You worry way too much, you know."

"I've got stuff on my mind."

"Oh, yeah? Like what?"

"Like where I should go next year. I'm thinking Simon Fraser because they'll probably cough up."

"Everyone's going to Trinity College. Come to Toronto."

"But the SFU scholarship covers everything. The Trinity one is more of an honorarium type thing."

"So? I'll get my dad to pay for it. BFD."

"I can't let your dad pay my tuition."

"Sure you can. Why not? It's a drop in the bucket."

"Because if I'm going to be powerful like him, I have to make it on my own."

I look over at him. "You're shooting

yourself in the foot doing things the hard way, you know."

"You've got it all figured out, don't you?"

"All I know is Trinity's going to be awesome. Girls, parties, clubs, all that jazz."

"The stuff I can't afford to distract myself with if I want to have a hope in hell of graduating."

"I'm telling you, you think too much."

I pull into his driveway. His grandma is on the lopsided front porch choosing potatoes from a large Tupperware tub. She waves. I grab Tom's jacket from one of the bags on the backseat and stick it on his lap. He doesn't want to take it and tries not to, but I force it on him. It's like my dad says, if you shove something at someone long enough, they take it. Especially if it's something they want.

"One day I'll be rich and powerful like your dad, and I'll get you back. You'll see."

Tom says the funniest things. I guess that's why they let a few regular people come to Montrose. It's entertaining.

"Look, whatever happens you can always come and crash on my floor next year," I say, punching his arm. "You've got that good sleeping bag you like to brag about. Bring that and live in my residence for free."

"Whatevs, man." He rolls his eyes and hops out.

Chapter 2

Animals

Up at six. We're headed for Whistler on the annual grade twelve ski trip. Mostly everyone's parents have property up there. Mine do. But the Montrose people think it's better if we stay together. Tom thought he couldn't go since we weren't going to be staying for free at my parents' condo, but I told him to come and crash with me at the hotel. I didn't tell him that I paid for his spot in the room. It really makes no difference to me to skim a little off the old trust fund, but I can't tell him I did it or he'll freak out. I don't get that guy sometimes. He lets the weirdest stuff bother him.

Mom throws some protein bars and coconut water at me before I leave the house. "I'm so glad you guys are getting carted up by bus this time," she says. "I don't want to deal with another crashed Jeep, like last time."

"I know, I know," I say. I'm so sick of hearing about that. Okay, so I went a little faster than the limit. Who doesn't? Was it really my fault there was a fallen log on the highway? I mean, it's got to be someone's job to keep that Sea-to-Sky route clear. "I'll stay out of trouble."

"That's my boy," she says. She points to her cheek. I give her a quick peck and head out.

Tom and I get to school by seven so we can get good seats at the back of the school bus. You always want to be at the back when it comes to things like this. It's kind of stupid that we all have to drive up together, but I guess this way I can enjoy the view.

* * *

We are somewhere just before Britannia Beach. I'm looking out at the Pacific Ocean when all of a sudden, the chatter gets real quiet. Everyone shuts up because Riaz Erzad and Yasmin Alvarez are talking. Yasmin and Riaz have been "in love" for the past nine or ten months. I never noticed much about Yasmin, but Riaz is a douche. The kind that wears way too much cologne and stinks up the halls.

I wasn't listening, so I didn't catch the first part, but the content is unmistakable when Riaz says, "You can't just hook up with other guys and expect everything will stay the same."

Yasmin protests, "I didn't."

"There's a video, okay?" Riaz's tone is kind of threatening. "I've seen the footage."

So maybe the rumour about the party the week before is actually true. Tom and I weren't there, so what do I know? But I heard some stuff went down. I'm always surprised when I hear stuff about girls like Yasmin, good girls. It's hard to think of her as the type to make out at all, never mind with guys who aren't her boyfriend.

"It was just a stupid game we were playing," she insists really loudly.

"Yeah, well, it looked like your mouth was where it shouldn't have been."

Even though we're on a bus with loud brakes, you can hear a pin drop. No one looks at them. It's like we all want to give them space, but there is no space since they've chosen to have this super-ugly scene in front of a captive audience. Tom and I look at each other. We both know what this means. They're officially broken up.

It isn't long before Yasmin moves to the only empty seat on the bus — right near us. I hear her sniffling, and when I take a quick glance, I see she's quietly sobbing into the sleeve of her hoodie. It's like seeing a turtle stuck on its back, and you just want to set it right-side up again. I know Tom has liked Yasmin forever, but never had the nads to go for it. I gesture to him to switch seats with me so he can go sit beside her or at least put his hand on her shoulder. Something. Instead he sits there looking tense.

The dudes at Riaz's end of the bus are loud-talking about how they're going to test drive Ferraris next weekend. One guy is convinced he's destined to drive a Bugatti.

If Tom isn't going to do anything, I have to.

"Hey, Yasmin," I say in a hushed voice.

"What?" she snaps, turning toward me, ready to respond if I say something mean.

"You're better off without him. The guy's a jerk."

I don't care if Riaz hears. He's been that way as long as I've known him, always strutting around school like he owns the place just because he's got better facial hair than anyone else.

Yasmin smiles a little. "Thanks."

"Yeah," Tom agrees, finally chiming in. "You deserve way better."

"You guys are sweet," she says and turns back around. She gets out her ear buds and an oversized orange toque and retreats into her own sad world.

* * *

When we pull into Whistler Village, the bus stops in front of the Fairmont. The whole group of us assembles out in front of the luggage compartment. Ms. Carmichael, our school's odd little math teacher who wears these old-fashioned floral sweaters, gives us her best loudspeaker voice.

"Now listen up. We trust you to behave yourselves, but remember that you're all responsible for your actions up here. No drinking. No drugs. No partying and staying up all hours of the night."

That gets a few laughs, the way she talks.

"I mean it," she says in an earnest voice. "Don't forget you signed contracts saying you'd behave yourselves or be sent home."

As she is speaking, Raoul Simon is literally climbing a wall behind her. There's this decorative touch where some big nails are sticking out of the stucco finish, and Raoul is scaling it like he's rock climbing in a gym. Ozzie and Kayla are running around high-jumping up into the Canadian flags that are planted along the sides of the Fairmont. Ms. Carmichael is in for a cold hard dose of reality: we're animals. We are beasts who will run wild at the first chance we get.

Chapter 3

Mountain Madness

Sneaking out of the hotel is nothing. After the teachers escort us to our six-person suites and tell us to stay put, they go down to the lobby to drink wine and gush over the chocolate fountain. All we have to do is leave through the back. Easy.

Evening darkness descends upon Whistler Village and the pubs light up with anticipation. Pop and rock music fills the main roads. Even though I grew up going to Whistler, going out on the town is new. When you come up with your parents, it sort of cramps your style.

There are rosy-cheeked girls as far as the eye can see. Every pub is filled with people having fun.

I gesture to Tom to head into the Amsterdam.

"Aren't they going to want to see some kind of proof that we're nineteen? Which we aren't."

"Quit bumming me out. We're supposed to be having fun."

"Whatever."

Inside, a hostess who looks like a supermodel takes us to a table for four. That's promising. If beer ads have taught me anything, it's that girls come to your table if you're having a good time, so a couple of extra seats will be handy.

"Your server will be right with you," says the supermodel, leaving behind a couple of menus.

Soon enough a guy comes over and introduces himself as Kevin. He squats down next to us to tell us about the specials.

"All right," he says, standing. "Can I get you guys started with something to drink?"

"Yeah, Heineken for me," I say. Kevin nods, then looks at Tom.

"How about a margarita bulldog?"

That's a drink featured on the glossy cardboard sign on our table. It's the flashiest drink you can imagine — a giant glass of green slush with a bottle of Corona turned upside-down into it, sticking out like a huge light bulb. I shoot him a look. Could he be any more amateurish?

"Sounds good," the server says. "I just gotta check your IDs."

Tom acts like he's annoyed, like this is some huge inconvenience, which is the exact kind of over-acting that usually backfires.

"My dad's got a tab here," I explain as I casually lean back on my chair. "We always get to drink. No one's ever asked for IDs before."

"Sorry, man, I gotta run this by my manager," Kevin says. "Hang tight. I'll be right back."

Hang tight? Is this guy for real?

Tom is beaming across the table. "I can't wait to try that bulldog. Looks awesome."

"Yeah," I say. I breathe deeply and look around the pub. At least there aren't any teachers around.

After what seems like forever, Kevin comes back.

"Sorry, man. You guys are underage. I can't let you drink."

"Let *me* talk to the manager."

"She just left. I'm shift supervisor, and I'm sorry but I can't authorize this. It's against the law."

"Call my dad. Seriously. He'll sort it out."

"Sorry, man."

I push my chair out in an abrupt way. People look. I didn't mean to do it that hard.

"I hope you liked this job, because you

won't have it much longer," I tell Kevin. Then I turn to Tom. "Let's get out of here."

He shrugs and follows me out.

"What a douche. I'm calling that manager first thing tomorrow."

Tom shrugs. "So, what now? Want to go to 7-Eleven for taquitos?"

"I want to go someplace rocking. This is supposed to be our big ski trip. I want to get drunk and pick up chicks and do all the stuff we've been planning."

"Yeah, well. I'm hungry."

"We can always go to Araxi, where they know me. For sure they won't check IDs."

"Isn't that some kind of fine dining place?"

"Yeah, my dad brings people there all the time, so we don't even have to pay."

"Even better," Tom says. "Do they have nachos?"

"I doubt it. More like these weird towers of food that you sort of have to knock over to eat."

"Then let's stop in at 7-Eleven first."

We make a detour for junk food. My stomach growls. No matter what the night holds, some nachos with that fake cheese sounds pretty good right about now.

Just as we come out with our bags of chips and snacks and vitamin water, Tom stops in his tracks. Across the way, Yasmin is smoking a cigarette. I didn't know she was a smoker.

"I wonder what she's doing out all by herself," Tom says.

"Maybe she wants to be alone."

"Yeah, right." Tom gives me a skeptical look.

"Dumped and friendless in Whistler Village. Sounds like a real after-school special," I joke.

"I have to talk to her, but what do I say?" Tom asks.

"Let me handle it."

She's staring at her phone, facing some well-pruned shrubs in a planter outside a boutique hotel. Ringlets of dark, curly hair flow out the front of her orange toque. She isn't wearing makeup or anything.

"Hey, Yasmin," I say, putting my hand on her shoulder.

She turns around. Her eyes are glassy, like she's been crying. I totally regret reaching out. It would've been a lot better to ignore her.

"Oh, hey." She wipes her eyes with the back of her sleeve. "What are you nerds doing?"

I don't want to tell her we're going to some old-people restaurant, so I improvise. "Ditching the village. You want to come?"

"You have a condo up here?"

I nod.

"Sure." She shrugs.

"Awesome," Tom and I say in unison, proving that — at least around girls — he is kind of a nerd. Whatever. As long as she doesn't get too emotional, it'll be fine.

"You got booze?" Yasmin asks. It's a

surprise to me that she drinks too, but I guess girls don't usually hook up with guys who aren't their boyfriends unless they're drinking. I guess she's not as innocent as she seems.

I nod. "I think there's some cider in the fridge."

"Is it peach? That's the only kind I like."

"Actually, I think it is."

"Right on," she says, smiling for the first time.

Right on, indeed. Easy. That's how you do it.

I look at Tom, feeling proud. We start walking toward the condo.

Yasmin's cool. She makes you feel like you're exactly where you're supposed to be. She doesn't giggle or flirt.

"Why do people call you Worm, anyway?" Yasmin asks Tom as we saunter through the village.

Tom shrugs. "Because they're morons?"

"I think it's because he can wriggle out of everything," I say. I want to talk him up more, just so she doesn't think we're total freaks, so I add, "Or maybe it's because he's close to the earth and likes camping."

"Aren't worms invertebrates?" Yasmin asks.

"I've got plenty of backbone, if that's what you mean," Tom says. "But I've got nothing against worms. They've been around a lot longer than us, and they'll be here after we're gone."

"Philosophical," Yasmin says, laughing. He should have gone with the camping thing. Or wriggling.

Chapter 4

Cake

My parents' condo looks pretty slick when I turn the light on. I don't understand why Mom insisted on getting that huge house in Kadenwood, a twenty-minute drive from the village. I think she wants us to sell this place when the other one is fully built, but this condo is right in the heart of everything. My mom calls this place my dad's "man cave" because of the ten-year-old leather couches and the hot tub on the deck.

I head straight for the fridge. Inside there's everything from French champagne to imported beer to the pink, girly strawberry rhubarb vodka coolers that my sister likes.

Thanks, Mom!

Tom hooks up his iPhone to the speakers and puts on some chill music.

"Anyone want a beer?" I call.

"Sure," Tom answers.

"Yasmin, I've also got a bunch of different brands of cider here, if you want to have a look."

As I pop off the caps from the beer bottles, Yasmin comes into the kitchen and peers into the fridge. When she's standing so close to me, there's this hint of coconut from her hair that reminds me of being at the beach, even in the dead of winter. I start picturing bikinis and girls' volleyball and, well, it's hard to think.

She reaches into the back of the fridge for a peach cider. She hands it to me to uncap, and when I pass it back, our fingers brush for just a second. She smiles. I make a mental note to tell Tom to go for another girl.

"You want a glass or anything?" I ask.

"Nah. I'm pretty low maintenance."

I don't know why, but when she turns, I put my hand on the small of her back to guide her to the living room, as if she hadn't just been there.

"After you," I say.

"Thanks," she replies. She tosses her dark curls over her shoulder in a sassy way that sends more tropical aroma in my direction.

"Now what?" Tom asks.

"Now we hang," I say. "So, Yasmin," I begin. "You into skiing?"

"Totally," she says. "I've gone every winter for as long as I can remember."

"You must be pretty good, then."

"I'm not bad," she says, and takes a sip. "I don't always get to ski as much as I want because we take turns staying with my sister. She's got cerebral palsy. She loves the mountains, though."

I don't really know what to say to that.

"But have you skied Whistler?" I ask.

"A couple of times," she says with a kind of bravado.

"What's the biggest run you've done?"

"I did the Saddle."

"Wow. Not bad."

"You?" The look in her eyes dares me to brag, so I do.

"Doom and Gloom, Frog Hollow and Stefan's Chute. That was a good one. Oh, and Cockalorum. But my favourite thing is chasing powder."

"You mean going out of bounds?"

I nod.

Tom gives me a look like I should quit talking to her in a language he doesn't understand, especially since she clearly likes it, but I can't help myself.

"Have you ever?" I ask.

"Backcountry? Sure. Not here, though. At Grouse."

"Grouse is a kiddie hill."

"Yeah, I know." She kind of pouts.

"Does anyone want some chips or something?" Tom interrupts. Yasmin and I look at him.

"I could eat," I say coolly.

Tom gets up and goes to the freezer. "There's pizza."

He pulls it out and turns on the oven. With him way on the other side of the room, it's even harder not to move in close to Yasmin. She's clearly passionate about skiing. Or is it me?

"We should do it on this trip," I say.

"Do what?" Tom asks from afar.

"Go for the powder," Yasmin says. She's reading my mind.

"Yeah, right," Tom says. "Like there's any getting away from Ms. Carmichael tomorrow."

His comment hangs in the room like a

fart. But he doesn't seem to notice.

"Twenty minutes oughta do it," Tom says, setting the timer on the oven.

He comes back and doesn't even try to sit closer to Yasmin.

"If they catch us, they'll totally suspend us. Or expel us," Yasmin says.

"But it'd be awesome," I say. "You can't argue with that. It'd be the coolest way to leave high school and forever remember our final year."

"I'm sick of doing everything by the rules," she says. "Riaz is a rule follower too, and it drove me nuts."

"So, what happened with you guys, anyway?" Tom asks.

"You mean the video?" She rolls her eyes. "It's totally stupid. I don't really want to talk about it."

"You don't have to," Tom says.

"It was seriously just camera angles and editing. You can do anything on iMovie."

So Riaz blew up at her for no reason. He did the same thing to me on the rugby field.

Friggin' guy.

"The thing that pisses me off is how quickly people will believe some stupid gossipy back-bitey thing and turn on you," she continues. "I mean, even my own friends think I did it."

"That sucks," Tom says. He's using open body posture like he's some kind of peer counsellor.

"What bugs me is it's all fake. I'm in the doghouse for nothing. So, I've been thinking, if I'm doing the time, I might as well do the crime."

Now it's getting interesting. "What do you mean?" I ask. "You want to make out with some guy?"

Right then, the oven timer goes off. Tom hesitates before going into the kitchen. When he's got the pizza all dished out on plates, I turn on the TV and pull up our Netflix options.

At midnight or so, we make our way back to the Fairmont where we're supposed to wake up the next morning. Yasmin walks between me and Tom the whole way.

"You know what, you guys?" she asks, sounding oddly peppy.

"What?" Tom asks.

"I have made a huge life choice tonight. I've been punished for eating cake that I didn't really eat. So I'm going to eat cake. I'm going to find a hot guy and rock his world. And when I do, I'll find a way to let you two know."

"I don't know, Yasmin," Tom says. "Maybe hold off on your life choices until the cider wears off."

"I say do whatever makes you feel good." That's my contribution.

Chapter 5

Hook Up

Tom slides the credit-card-style key into the
lock of our suite. We're being quiet, since
the other guys we share the room with are
probably asleep. But as soon as we open the
door, it turns out that's not even a little bit
true. There's an action movie on and everyone's
sitting around looking at their phones. Since
there's six of us, it's a good thing we got the
presidential suite, which has three different
bedrooms. But even though the place is big, it

feels tight and it stinks of sports equipment.

I hurl myself onto the bed near Tom's in the room we're sharing, the one in the middle with a view of the village.

"Where were you guys?" Ozzie asks from the couch.

"Drinking."

"Where?"

"My parents' condo."

"Oh." He sounds disappointed. "I thought you were going to say you went out."

"We weren't here, were we?" I snap. "That's out."

Ozzie goes back to looking at his phone and semi-watching the movie.

I think about flirting with Yasmin. I wish I was alone so I could really get off on it. But Tom is in the bathroom next door, and I can't get it up with the other guys belching and farting in the next room.

As if he could hear my thoughts, Tom comes out of the bathroom in his PJs and gets on his bed.

"Tomorrow's gonna be insane," I say.

He nods. "You don't really think Yasmin's going to ditch out with us, do you?"

"What's that about Yasmin?" Ozzie asks.

Tom and I look at him.

"Never mind, man."

"All right," he says in a way that suggests it's anything but all right. He's always trying to get in on whatever we do. Not that I mind if it's something like going out for lunch or whatever, but we don't need any extra pressure tomorrow. It's hard enough choreographing an escape for three.

I turn to Tom. "She'll be there."

Suddenly, my phone vibrates. It's past midnight so I figure it's my mom having one of her helicopter parent moments, freaking out that I'm away from home because it means she's old. But when I check, it's from a number I don't recognize.

Hey, it's Yasmin. Meet me downstairs?

How'd she get my number? This is my first thought. My second thought is: *Hurry up and get downstairs.* Third thought: *Should I tell Tom?* Fourth thought: *No way.* I get out of bed and grab my hoodie.

"Where are you going?" Tom asks.

"I need some air."

"Now?"

"I'll be back in five."

* * *

In the Fairmont lobby, I see Yasmin. She's wearing lip gloss and she's also in her pyjama bottoms with a hoodie up top. The dim lighting makes her shiny lips gleam. I can't stop staring. She has full-on porn lips.

"What's up?" I ask, sitting down next to her on the couch in the lobby. It's weird being down here at this hour. The concierge guy isn't even here. He's probably sleeping out back.

"Did I wake you up?" she asks.

"No."

"I just was thinking . . ." she says in a soft faraway whisper.

"Oh, yeah? About what?"

"About cake, and about you."

"About *me*?"

"You're cute."

"I am?"

She nods and looks away. Her weird blend of shyness and straightforwardness makes me want to grab and kiss her.

"So, you're tired of being a good girl?" I ask.

"Totally."

"And that's why you are texting me to come meet you in the middle of the night?"

"I'm sick of being the person I've been all my life. Half Catholic, half Muslim. Accountable to every God known to mankind. I'm over it."

"What do you mean, you're over it?"

"I mean, I'm sick of doing everything right. I liked what you said earlier about doing what feels good. You're good at that."

"At what?"

"Thinking about yourself. I need to stop living up to everyone else's expectations and just do more of what I want to do."

"And what do you want to do right now?" I ask, touching her arm. She gives me that look girls give you when they want you to kiss them. I lean in and before I know it, it's happening.

The concierge makes a lot of coughing noises when he comes out from the back room. We stop, but then Yasmin takes me by the hand and we head into the elevator. She pushes the emergency stop and we kiss some more. I pin her against the wall of the elevator and her moans tell me she's into it. Before I know it, we are really getting into it. I mean, like, *really, really*. She slips her hand into my pyjama pants and maybe it's a good thing I didn't get a chance for a quick tug in the suite. Next thing I know, she kneels. I can't look away. Her mouth is so warm.

When she finally pulls away and pushes the elevator button to my floor, I swear I have no brain cells left at all. I can't believe I just hooked up with Yasmin Alvarez. That makes three girls in my graduating class.

"That was fun," she says. "Goodnight."

"Goodnight yourself," I say, giving her a final kiss on the cheek.

Back in the room, I try not to show any emotion at all. I don't want to give anything away, especially to Tom. There's just no point.

* * *

When the alarm sounds in the morning, it feels as though I've only just fallen asleep.

"Get up. Get up," Sean says.

There's a round of moaning and groaning.

Before long, there's a knock at the door. "Downstairs in twenty!"

It's Ms. Carmichael. She sounds grumpy but the day is bright. The sun is streaming in around the gaps of the dark, drawn curtains. I go over to the window and pull the long, eighties-style curtains to the side.

A round of protests sounds from the still-sleepy skiers.

Then Raoul yells out, "Whistler!"

A horde of half-naked dudes cram into the bathroom to shower and brush their teeth. It's a jungle in there as we all grab for whatever we need. Everyone gets splashed. The towels all end up on the ground. No one even considers taking turns. So you have one guy taking a dump, while another takes a shower and a third brushes his teeth.

We pile into the elevator and then into the restaurant where Ms. Carmichael says we have fifteen minutes before we all head out together. The buffet table looks like a feeding trough, and I run into the action, grab a plate and go at the scrambled eggs with abandon. I am starving.

Chapter 6

Howling

I don't see Yasmin in the dining room, which is a relief because I don't really know what to say to her. I hope she doesn't want to talk about feelings or going out or anything. Tom and I go outside to wait for the rest of the class. We loiter out in front of the lodge, and sure enough, a puff of smoke comes out from behind one of the potted shrubs.

"Bet that's her," I say.

Tom heads over. This time it's me who's

not so sure. What if she acts like we're together? Still, I have no choice but to follow.

She looks pretty rough, like she didn't sleep at all, but she smiles when she sees us. "Oh, hey."

"Mornin'," Tom says like he's some kind of cowboy.

"How was your night?" I ask.

"Ugh. Terrible." She takes a long drag off her cigarette and lets the butt fall to the ground. "You know what sucks ass? Having to sleep in the same room as a chick who's in love with the jerk who dumped you."

"Brutal," Tom says. "But you gotta move on. Stop going out with jerks."

"Yeah," I agree.

"Riaz is a good guy," she snaps. She puts out her cigarette by smooshing it under her shiny, black ski boot and sticks her hand in her pocket. "Look at me. Still trying to convince myself he's decent. Our families know each other. There's all this pressure on me to like him."

"Were you guys supposed to get an arranged marriage or something?" I ask. I regret the question as soon as it's out of my mouth.

Yasmin scoffs. "No!" She looks at me like I'm a moron.

Meekly, she adds, "Well, not officially. I dunno. My parents wouldn't be sad about it, let's put it that way. But I don't know if that whole marriage deal is for me, anyway."

"It isn't?" Tom asks.

She looks totally pissed. "I didn't say it *wasn't*. I said I don't know. I don't want to spend my life picking up some guy's underwear, all right?"

Awkward. Silence. We all look around.

"So, who's into Riaz?" Tom wants to know.

Yasmin's glare tells me she's not going to be giving anything up. I respect that, just like I respect her not coming at me with hugs and hand-holding and all that stuff that sometimes goes along with hooking up. Besides, I don't really care about who likes Riaz.

"Anyway, are we still on? You know . . . with the plan?" I ask.

"I dunno. My stomach's kinda . . ." She makes a vomitty sort of face while teeter-tottering her hand back and forth.

I ignore her and yell out, "Whistler!" just like Raoul had earlier.

It's like howling at the moon, declaring that we're here at last.

She smiles at me. "It's fun to be you, isn't it?" she asks.

I shrug. "I have a good time."

She shakes her head like she's making fun of me, but I don't think she is.

"He lives the good life," Tom adds. "He's got it easy."

"Why? Because I like to enjoy myself?" I ask. It comes out more defensive than I mean it to. "You guys can yell out, too, if you want."

"But we don't," Yasmin says. They exchange glances.

"So don't," I say, trying to understand what the big deal is. "Let's get going."

The rest of the class and the teachers catch up to us, and together, like a swarm of flies but less coordinated, we make our way over to the gondola, gear slung up on our shoulders. It's a cool sight, that's for sure. I want to yell again, but I hold back.

Everyone flocks through the gates to the gondolas and starts piling in.

"Only six to a car," the attendant says. She's all serious and in her twenties. School trips are obviously not her favourite thing to deal with. She scowls her way through it and sticks her arm straight out, police-style, to make us stop.

I don't mind when she holds Tom and me back, since we were about to be shoved into the car with the dudes from the room. I am kind of sick of their stench by now.

The next one comes by, and the grumpy attendant ushers us in.

Yasmin is the last one on ours.

Now we have thirty minutes to kill as we slowly make our ascent to the peak of the mountain that has seen Olympic champions win gold medals. The mountain air is cool as it whooshes in through the small open window at the top of the gondola. Yasmin stands up and holds onto the bar. She stares out at the scenery below and I wonder what is going through her mind.

I want to put my arms around her like I did last night. Does she want that, too? Or is she being shy because she woke up and realized she made a mistake? Her silence is killing me.

The stillness of the ride is broken by two girls I barely know.

"Harmony Ridge, here we come," Celeste says.

"I can't wait," her friend answers and whispers something into her ear. They're having their own little party, or maybe they're just too snobby to include the rest of us.

Yasmin has this faraway look in her eyes, like she's present, but not. She's living in a private world that we're not a part of and she ignores the small talk. She stares into the distance.

We get out at the top, and even though I've been up the mountain many, many times, this is different. I grab my skis and poles off the side of the car and toss them over my shoulder. The air is fresher, more intoxicating. The brightness of the sun's reflection off the snow mirrors my mood completely. I am all shine.

We make our way off the gondola platform to the crunchy snow outside. Already, the guys ahead of us are making morons of themselves on the Olympics podium, posing like they've won medals, then mooning the cameras.

"Time to hit the rentals," Tom says. He trudges off through the snow over to the small wooden cabin that outfits people in gear. I think about how many stinky feet have been in those boots. I don't know how he can live with it. Yasmin fishes a pack of cigarettes from her jacket pocket and walks over to the railing to smoke and survey the landscape.

"I'll wait here," I say. I notice this huge wooden carving of an eagle. Its beak is knocked off. I try to imagine what happened. Probably some teenaged hooligans like us rammed into it. Who knows? But it looks weird, that big injured bird.

Chapter 7

No Limits

The chill in the air stings my cheeks. There's nothing better than being at the peak of a gigantic mountain in the middle of winter.

"Listen up, everyone," Ms. Carmichael says, then blows a whistle.

Mr. Svendson, the biology teacher, takes over. "Well, folks. We're finally here. Everyone let out a big cheer."

Boy, do we. I think we frighten a flock of tourists with our enthusiasm.

"Just a reminder that this out here —" he gestures all around him "— this is wilderness, people. There are bears and cliffs and real dangers. We want you to have fun, but we also need you to be safe. No one goes off alone. No one strays from the trails. No one goes beyond the limits of their skill level. Capiche? Now, we've got a diverse bunch this year. Some of you have never skied before and you'll go with Ms. Carmichael. And some of you are pretty advanced. You'll stay here with me."

The teachers get us divided up into groups, and just then, chaos descends over the group. People split up every which way. That's when Tom and I look at each other.

"Now or never," I say.

"Let's get out of here," Tom says.

"Wait for me."

We turn. It's Yasmin, coming up behind us.

"We're really doing it, aren't we?" she asks.

"Hell yeah!" I say.

"Then we better hurry. Mr. Svendson will

notice before too long."

The air is so cool and brisk it makes my throat feel like a wind tunnel. The brightness is blinding as we ski up to the second lift that will take us all the way to the top.

Yasmin says, "Want to sit with me?" as we make our way to the front of the line. Three is such an awkward number. No way do I want to talk about what happened last night, especially with Tom just one seat away from us, so I can't take the chance.

"Why don't you two go first?"

Alone, I watch them from my seat. Tom puts his arm around her. *Good luck with that.*

Even though Tom's my best friend, I don't want Yasmin to like him. I kind of want her to like me. And I'm sort of convinced that she does. It's not that I want to go out with her. I don't. But I could go for another late-night hook up or ten.

We ski off the lift platform and make our way over toward the slalom run.

"I gotta take a leak," Tom says, and gestures for me to join him.

We're behind some trees, standing side by side, and Tom says, "Maybe we should just stick to the regular runs."

"We can't turn back now," I say. "Aren't you trying to get Yasmin to like you?"

"I think maybe she kinda does."

"Then you really need to do this. Trust me. It's that whole 'living life on the edge' thing. Girls like that."

"Whatever," Tom says. I can tell he thinks I am full of shit and maybe I am, but the air is so crisp and we've come all this way.

"It's too late to go back and find Mr. Svendson anyway," I add. I just don't understand Tom's attitude. It's like he's determined to see life through the eyes of someone who's defeated or something. What's the worst that can happen? It's just snow after all. We're surrounded by acres and acres of soft snow.

We keep going. Farther and farther into

the back caverns of the mountain, we hike. The snow is fresh and untouched, and ours are the first and only tracks in it. As far as the eye can see is nothing but wilderness.

"Up ahead!" I call to them.

They both turn and look my way.

I point. "Over there."

There's a perfect spot. I go toward it, not wanting to look back too often. I also don't want to go too fast in case Yasmin actually wants to be up front with me. I have to give her a chance to make another move, right?

We finally arrive at this break in the trees. I look over the side of the steep mountain, and sure enough, there's a white path below us, perfectly untouched. From my backpack I pull out my phone. It's time for a quick selfie and group shot.

"Wait," Yasmin says, reaching into her pocket. She puts on tinted lip balm that makes her even more kissable. What I wouldn't give to be there with her alone. I start to imagine what we'd get up to, and then quickly force myself to concentrate on setting up the picture instead. No distractions.

To avoid staring at Yasmin, I scan the horizon. Far away, just past the lift that goes all the way up to the peak of the mountain, you can see these tiny black ants slaloming down the white slide. They could be our classmates. It's impossible to tell. We're way over on the other side of the mountain, doing the unthinkable.

I never say this, but the conditions are perfect. That other snow that the class is on has been so trekked out. This stuff in front of us is pure powder. I pick up a handful of it and blow. The flakes go everywhere. I laugh so hard the other two give me looks, but Yasmin smiles and I can tell she's a snow snob, too.

She follows my lead and kicks some up. "It's so light," she says.

"Incredible," Tom agrees as though he knows what he's talking about. He's such an open book, that guy. It's obvious he's still tripping out over whether we should be here at all, but I know he'll thank me when we're back in the village.

It was like this the first time we took our dirt bikes down Seymour. He was terrified, but then he was on cloud nine when it was all over. I guess that's life. You don't get the highs if you aren't a little afraid. Even I have a bit of hesitation. Looking out over the vista, we see nothing but snow-capped mountains and white trees, and there's that silence. Winter perfection.

"So? Who's first?" I ask.

"Here?" Yasmin asks, pointing with her pole. The path starts with a jump. "That's kind of steep," she says.

"This ain't Grouse," I answer, nodding with confidence. "It'll be a killer run."

"You go," Tom says to me.

"Okay," I say. "Here goes nothing."

With that, I launch, and I swear, I fly. I

can feel the thrill in my stomach. Never have I known snow so soft, so ready for me. I gain speed as I go, swishing my way between trees and down the side of the mountain, far out of view of anyone. My body is light, and every little movement makes a huge difference. I stay in toward the mountain, like I'm clinging to its side as I make my way around the edge. I am deep into feeling my hips and shoulders working together like a machine. It's the perfect moment, like the world is standing still just for me to have this experience.

Just when the slope angles in a way that slows me down, I hear a scream.

Chapter 8

Disaster

As though on command, my neck cranes and I halt. That was Yasmin! That horrible sound — the sound of real trouble — reverberates through the air. It's followed by deafening silence pierced only by the sound of the wind.

She's nowhere. There's nothing to see but trees and the painful brightness of the sun's rays on the snow.

I pull out my phone, text her and wait.

Nothing. I text Tom to see if he's heard, but he doesn't answer either.

I have to go back.

I unlatch my skis and fling them up over my shoulder. Then I make my way up the slope I've just gone down, retracing my path slowly. The snow is deep and I sink into it.

"Marcus!" It's Tom but I can't see him. He calls me again.

"Where are you?" I cry out.

"Over here."

I finally get a visual. He's splayed out, like a fly that's been swatted against a wall. One ski is several metres away. And he's lying in the snow.

"Dude," I call out. "Let's get you up."

I run to him, sinking into the snow with each step but determined to get there. Everything is in slow motion. My legs can barely carry me; I am that heavy. It is as though I am watching it all happen from somewhere far away.

When I get closer, the sunlight refracts off two streams of tears that run down Tom's face. Involuntary, I guess. He's in pain. That's obvious.

"Come on," I say, holding my hand out to him when I'm finally within reach. "Let's get you standing."

"Dude. I can't feel my legs."

"You're cold," I say. That's happened to me before. Heck, it's happened to every skier.

"I don't know about that. Something snapped."

"You're imagining it."

I tell myself he overdramatizes everything.

"Nah, man. Like, I can't move my legs."

"You have to," I insist. My voice is like Ms. Carmichael's, demanding and loud.

"I can't." I've never seen his face like this before. Hopeless.

"Do you want to die out here?" I ask, sounding like some kind of military officer.

"I don't know. Maybe."

"Come on, man. Take my hand."

He reaches for me and I pull him, but he really cannot stand.

"Holy shit. Tom." That's when it hits me that this is actually happening. It's real. My mind blanks on Yasmin as I focus on my best friend, like I'm trying to get him out of the jaws of a bear or shark.

"You have to get help," Tom says.

"On it." I whip out my phone. I hadn't thought to put the Whistler emergency on my phone. *Idiot.* I call 911. As I explain the issue, the operator keeps getting me to repeat myself. She refuses to believe it, too, I guess.

"You're . . . where?" she asks in that tone that mothers use when they can't understand how stupid their children are. "What run are you on, exactly?"

I tell her we're in backcountry.

"Help is on the way, but it'll be a while. You're going to need to stay with Tom. And for the love of God, don't try to move him."

"I'll be here." I don't want to say that I already moved him.

"Is anyone else with you?"

"Yeah. Her name is Yasmin Alvarez."

"And where is she?"

Should I tell her about the scream?

"I don't know. I think she may have crashed as well."

"Well, stay put. Wait for the rescue crew and you can explain to them."

Once I'm off the phone, Tom looks at me. The wind blows snowflakes onto his face. I wish he could stand up. It's not so bad if you're standing.

"Where the hell is Yasmin?" he asks.

"Did you hear her scream?" I ask.

"Yeah. She was behind me. When I turned to look, that's when I hit the tree that sent me tumbling forward. I landed on that pointy rock over there, then tumbled over here."

"Oh, God," I say. *Oh God. Oh God. Oh God.*

"You gotta go look for her."

"The 911 lady said to stay here with you."

"I'm fine. You gotta find Yasmin."

I can't tell him that I can't do it. My legs are frozen solid; not from the cold but from total and utter dread at what I might find if I follow that scream. It was not the scream of a small accident. That was the terror call of someone facing what we all fear the most. I cannot go looking for her.

"What the hell is going to happen?" Tom asks. "What if . . . what if . . . this is really bad?"

"It won't be. You'll see." I have to stay positive. That's what my dad always says. No matter what life hands you, stay positive. *Breathe.* I can't breathe.

"But what if . . . ?" Tom's question trails off.

"Tom, chill. It'll be fine."

I even nod the way my dad does when he's trying to convince someone of something.

I've watched him do it in business. In vivid detail, I remember him telling me about the subconscious power of body language and how nodding puts people at ease and makes them agree with you. But what's the point of convincing people things will be fine when maybe they won't?

"I have a feeling she'd have texted us by now to tell us she was okay. I mean, if she really was okay," Tom says.

"She's okay," I say. I don't want him to panic. That's why I hold it together. "She's skied before."

"She was distracted. She just got dumped. She didn't eat breakfast. Oh, God."

"Stop freaking out," I order. I sound just like my dad that time I went to him with a scraped knee and gravel stuck in my bleeding gash. He didn't comfort me. He just yelled.

"Dude, she could be . . ." Tom stops talking and looks away.

"Quit it."

"But. That scream."

I refuse to consider any option that involves Yasmin not being okay. Yasmin is definitely okay. She has to be. She was right here two seconds ago.

I get a text from search and rescue telling me to stay calm and hold on. I am pretty sure that doesn't mean going off to look for Yasmin, but I also can't just hang out.

"I'm going to retrace her tracks."

"Yeah. Go."

Chapter 9

The Drop

I snap my skis into place and slowly move in the direction of the two thin lines that Yasmin left behind in the snow. She didn't follow my tracks. She went down, closer to the edge.

The slope is enticing, but I don't dare go fast. I snowplough the whole way. I start to understand what happened. The view is breathtaking. We're talking absolutely impossible to look away from, so maybe she didn't. Up ahead I see a cliff. It looks like it could be a mini one, that jumping off it would lead to landing in soft snow a few metres down, but something tells me there's more to this jump than meets the eye. I slow down even more, not daring to meet the same fate.

As I near the edge, I see a huge drop, one that would inspire the kind of scream that still rings in my ears. I cannot undo that sound. Peering over, I half-expect to see her broken body, like a scene in a movie, but it's too steep. No doubt she's down there somewhere, and I'm pretty sure she could not have survived a fall like that.

A pang of pain comes over me. I fall to my knees and let out a kind of howl I've never heard before. I'm not crying, exactly. It's something else. More like wailing. I'm kneeling exactly where Yasmin's tracks end.

It's too steep to make my way back with my skis on. Stepping up the mountain sideways is way too hard. I snap them off and carry them over my shoulder as I make the long climb back up to Tom.

Any other time, I wouldn't have been able to scale the angle of the mountain upwards. It's like those stories you hear of mothers who are able to lift up cars when their babies get stuck underneath. I know I have to get back to Tom, so I make it back, even though, logically, I never should have been able to. That's how steep it is on the path Yasmin took.

I see a crew of people in red jackets with white crosses on their backs surrounding Tom. I must have been gone longer than I thought. I am experiencing time in a really bizarre way. It's going both faster and slower than usual.

At first, they don't see me. I can tell they're busy trying to put Tom into one of the rescue toboggans. They huddle over him like football players.

From afar, one looks my way.

"Are you Marcus?"

"Yeah."

"We told you not to leave your friend.

Why did you leave?"

"I was only gone a minute."

We look at each other, both of us aware I am lying. A woman with pink cheeks and wrinkles says nothing. She stares at me with piercing green eyes.

"What were you guys thinking?" she asks, shaking her head. "Don't you know how dangerous it is out here?"

There's really no response to that. "Is Tom going to be all right?" I ask.

"That's not for us to say."

A man on a walkie-talkie yells into the speaker. "Patient is ready."

Far away there's a noise like a drum roll. It gets louder and louder. A helicopter appears from around the bend of the mountain. It must have come from the village. I can't believe it. In my mind, I imagined Tom being skied down on the sled. I thought it wouldn't be so bad. Maybe he'd broken a leg. It wouldn't be the first time.

But when the helicopter hovers and the paramedics attach the toboggan to it, I get scared. There's my best friend, suspended from a helicopter, tied by ropes. They're taking him to the emergency ward.

Then it hits me: it's me who put him in this situation. It's my fault.

The woman with the sunburned pink cheeks looks at me. Her eyes cannot conceal the anger she obviously feels.

"So, there was another skier with you?"

"Uh. Yeah. Yasmin Alvarez."

"Can you tell us where to look for her?"

I tell her about the drop.

I watch the helicopter ambulance take Tom away, while I stand like a statue. The rest of the rescue crew gather around me. They talk to each other, and two of them decide they're going to retrace Yasmin's trail.

The stern woman's face softens a bit, and she puts her hand on my arm and pats me.

"It's okay," she says, looking at me

watching Tom. "He's in good hands. He'll be okay. Let's get you down the mountain."

I nod, unable to say anything. "I'll see him down," she says to the others.

In silence, I ski down behind her. The woman slows now and then, looks back at me and gestures for us to keep going. Maybe she's worried I won't make it on my own if she doesn't escort me. Then she gets out her radio and talks in code. I don't remember breathing since the top of the mountain.

At the bottom, there's Ms. Carmichael. She's clutching her phone to her ear, and when she sees me, she turns it off and runs over.

"I'm glad you're okay," she says.

I notice she's shaking.

I still can't say anything. I can't cry. I can't smile or reassure her.

"Come here, let's get you to the bench," she says.

She talks to me the way the eldercare workers sometimes talk to my grandpa at the home. It's as though she thinks I am senile or not quite with it, and maybe she's right. For the first time in my entire life, I am in over my head. It's hard to even get to the closest bench because I am dizzy, my head is pounding and I realize that I am trembling.

When I finally sit down, the exhaustion really hits.

"Wait here, okay? Don't go anywhere."

"Okay," I say.

I have no idea where I would go. The only place I want to be is at home in my bed, but that world is very, very far away. I clutch my core like I'm in a straitjacket of my own making. I'm so cold my teeth are chattering.

Ms. Carmichael comes back to tell me that they found Yasmin's body. All I can do is stare at her.

Chapter 10

Nothingness

Filing an accident report at the mountain is awful. Giving my description of Yasmin and what happened is like reliving the nightmare. Inside me, I have this emptiness.

The officer is nice enough. He doesn't ask too many questions once he realizes I can't offer much information. Instead, he wants to know where my parents are and when they'll be home. I tell him my dad is on a business trip and my mom is probably out shopping. The truth.

Before I know it, I'm back in front of the Fairmont. Ms. Carmichael tosses my bag and equipment into a cab and tells the driver to bill the school. She reads the digits off a credit card. I'm in the backseat, looking out at the Pacific again, this time with no friends around, a splitting headache and blurred vision.

As it turns out, my mom is home. She's in front of the big screen TV in the living room doing her yoga.

"Marcus? That you?"

"Yep," I say, lugging my equipment past her to the stairs that lead up to my room.

"Why are you back so early?"

I can't get into it with her. There's no way I can face another two hours of her emotional reactions.

"I'm not feeling well."

"Is everything okay?" she asks.

That word again.

Nothing is okay. Okay is over.

"I'm just going to go lie down and sleep it off."

"Well, do you want some dinner?"

"Nah."

"Tylenol?"

"I already took some," I call from halfway up the stairs.

It's not like I sleep peacefully or anything. I close my eyes and the world kind of goes black and everything stops for a while. I can't make the sound of Yasmin's scream go away. When I open my eyes, it's morning and all I feel is dread.

I know it's wrong, but still I can't bring myself to tell my mom anything. It's as though I have this one tiny little window that shows what's left of her version of me. What I have to tell her is so disappointing and so ugly, she will look at me with a face that smacks of horror and say my name in the tone she used when I was ten and forgot to lock up my bike and got it stolen.

That's why I say nothing. I let her bring me food and drinks in my room. I let her sit by the side of my bed and feel my forehead like I am a kid again.

She's pretty, my mom. I don't really look at her most of the time, but since there are no words at all, and she's sitting quietly by my side, I notice it. She keeps herself up with lots of exercise and trips to the spa. She's always so manicured and put together, and I guess that's why I don't want to be the cause of her falling apart.

"Mom?" I start.

"What is it?"

"Nothing."

When she asks about the trip, I turn over and pretend I have a stomach ache.

✳ ✳ ✳

I clutch my phone and check social media. The first post I see is Yasmin's face surrounded by 's and RIPs. Kayla and that girl, Celeste, from the gondola have posted the "Do Not

Stand at My Grave and Weep" poem, like they did when Robin Williams died.

I have to see Tom. That's the only thing that gets me out of bed. After texting Tom's dad, I find out he's at Lions Gate Hospital. No point in showering. Jeans and a hoodie will do. Mom's gone, thank God, so I don't have to explain.

I get in my Jeep and drive to North Van. Finding his room is easier than I expected. All I have to do is ask. Then I walk those weird steps and take in that strangely scented, sterilized smell that masks the odour of sickness.

There's Ed Lee, right outside the room, talking on his phone. I am so close I can hear it's about a job. He says he can't take it for family reasons, and he quickly gets off the phone. He turns and sees me.

Face to face, I think for a second he wants to punch me. I think he should. If he knew the truth, he would. It's the first time in my entire life that I know what it is to be ashamed. I can barely look at him.

"Marcus," he says. He hugs me. "How could this happen?"

The man I've looked up to for years, the guy who taught me how to use a hammer and how to catch a fish, is crying.

"I'm so sorry," I say.

"It was an accident," Ed says, clutching me to him. The word haunts me.

"How's Tom?" I ask. I don't want to look at Ed, so I keep my gaze on the water fountain, then sniff up my runny nose and wipe it with my sleeve.

"Why don't you go in and see for yourself."

Tom's mom is at his bedside, and when she sees me, she gets up and hugs me, too. It's almost worse that they're nice to me.

"We should let you guys have a bit of time alone," she says.

She goes to Ed, who puts his arms around her as though he's sheltering her from a bomb, which is kind of what this is to the Lees.

"We're getting some coffee. You guys need anything?" Ed asks.

I shake my head.

"Iced tea?" Tom asks. I guess he can have just about anything he wants now.

His parents leave, and I sit down on the chair that's still warm from his mom's presence.

"So, it looks like I won't be walking again," Tom says.

"What? That can't be."

"That's what they say, the doctors here."

"Can't they do anything?"

"Remember how I told you I felt that snap? I guess that was my spine."

"But, Tom, it's impossible. They can fix everything nowadays."

"Apparently not." He looks at me with total seriousness, the kind I've never seen before. "Listen, I can't ask this question in front of my parents, but I need you to go ask one of the doctors whether I'm still working down there." He gestures at his lap. "I haven't had a second alone with anyone yet and I've got to know."

I understand exactly what he means. Like a man on a mission, I dart out to find a doctor. I'd want to know, too, if I were him. What would life be like without sex?

The doctor is easy to spot with her clipboard and laptop, sitting in the next room with another patient.

"Can I help you?" she asks when I barge in.

"Yeah, my friend Tom is in there," I say, pointing to his room. "He's got a spinal cord injury and we were kind of wondering if he was, you know, all right."

She gets up, excusing herself from the other patient. She steers me out of the room into the corridor. She picks up a chart from the plastic holder outside the door of Tom's room.

"Well, it's a pretty life-changing injury, to be honest."

"Yeah, yeah. I know. But what he really needs to know is whether he'll ever be able to . . ." I made a sort of rolling gesture with my hands, hoping she'll read between the lines. No luck. She just looks at me. I finally ask, "Will his dick still work?"

"Oh!" she says, as if I am finally speaking her language. She checks the folder with Tom's name on it. "It's too early to tell for sure, but it's possible. He's most likely functional. It'll be an adjustment, these things always are, but eventually he'll learn the mechanics."

I go back into Tom's room and give him an immediate thumbs-up. He looks relieved. In spite of the good news, I don't know what to do with myself. It's like my eyes can't rest on anything because it's all so horrible, so I keep scanning the room looking for neutral objects like the light switch and the box of tissues on the bedside stand.

"You can fight this, Tom." The words sound stupid even as I say them, but I have to offer him something.

"I don't know, man. Maybe not this time."

"Don't give up."

"How's Yasmin? Did they find her?"

"You haven't checked your phone lately, have you?" I ask. There's no way to make what I'm about to say more pleasant, so I look him right in the eye. "She didn't make it."

"What?" His face goes totally pale. "I've been lying here thinking that I'll take whatever comes my way as long as she's all right. I can live with anything if she's still fine."

Of course Tom made bargains like that. Tom always puts the people he cares about ahead of himself. As I watch Tom's eyes well up, the tragedy that she's gone really hits home.

We sit in silence for a long time, and then his parents come back in with their coffee and a bottle for Tom. Ed is smiling, no doubt trying to cheer Tom up.

"Peach flavour okay?" he asks. Like Yasmin's peach cider.

"I can't have anything," Tom says, turning his head toward the window as if he wants to get away from us.

"What happened?" Mrs. Lee asks.

"Marcus just told me Yasmin Alvarez died."

Mrs. Lee makes a sound somewhere between a gasp and a sob.

Ed puts his arm around Tom. Tom looks up at me.

"Look, man, you better go," he says.

"I'll call you later?" I ask, getting up.

He doesn't answer.

I drive home in a daze. It's like all I have for a brain is a hamster in one of those little plastic balls. My thoughts tumble around all over the place and bang into walls and dead ends.

I thank God my mom still isn't home when I get there. If I go to bed early, I figure she'll think I've been in bed all day and not come asking any questions. And if I can sleep again, maybe I'll wake up and everything will be better. Everything will be easy, like it was before this weekend.

Chapter 11

Injustice

On Monday, in homeroom, the announcements come on.

"We regret to inform you that this year's ski trip to Whistler resulted in two tragedies. Homeroom is extended by ten minutes so your teachers can talk to you about it."

The teacher gets going, explaining how Tom Lee is in hospital with permanent injuries and that Yasmin Alvarez died in a fall from an unmarked cliff and her funeral will be this Saturday. Apparently a grief counsellor is coming to visit each of us individually, but no one is even listening to that part. It's like a blanket of fog has descended over us, like no one can see their own hands in front of them. They're clearly in shock, like I've been for the last forty-eight hours. Some look like they've already been crying, some gasp and check their phones, and others sit perfectly still with wide eyes, still not able to process the information.

Everyone asks me the same question.

"What happened?"

I get asked all over: in homeroom, in the hallways, and in my first class. I try to answer in detail. I feel like the only surviving soldier from a battle that exhausted me. I don't want to talk about it, but I feel like I owe people something.

"We went up past the lift and, well, the run wasn't an actual run, and so there were no markings to show that there was a cliff . . . And there were trees everywhere. They were easy to smack into if you weren't careful or if you were distracted."

I do not say that Tom was sidetracked by the scream. I don't want that scream to haunt anyone else. I think about Tom and wonder if he hears it in his dreams the way I do. That horrible sound has taken over my mind and I hear it even as I try to talk to my classmates. I realize I can never make them understand what happened. It's pointless to try.

I'm in Economics class when there's a knock at the door. Mr. Kim, my guidance counsellor, wants me to come with him. Maybe he's going to get all shrink-y on me and ask me about my childhood, or ask me what different-coloured ink blots look like to analyze how I'm coping.

I gather up my books and put them into my Herschel bag, and then I meet him out in the hallway.

"The principal wants to see you, Marcus."

"About?"

"The weekend."

Our footsteps sound so loud in the empty hallway; I don't want to ask anything else.

Mr. Kim holds the principal's door open for me. Mr. Bains, the principal, gestures to one of the chairs by his desk. I sit down. Mr. Kim takes the other chair.

"Marcus, I really don't have words for what has happened. When Ms. Carmichael told me about your involvement, I hesitated to call you in here. We're all grieving, but you must be going through some complicated emotions right now."

"Yeah," I manage.

"At this point, I think it's best if you take a few days to think about what happened. None of us are bigger than Mother Nature, Marcus. I'm not blaming you for what happened to Tom and Yasmin, but I want you to reflect on this."

"Okay."

"To be honest, I see no other option but to

cancel all future ski trips. This cannot happen again."

"Oh."

"And as soon as I get your statement, we'll start the process of expelling Tom."

"Wait. What?"

"Someone's taking the fall for this, Marcus. If you want to, go ahead and try, but I've dealt with your father's lawyers before."

"But it wasn't Tom's fault."

"Don't try to be noble now. It's too late."

"But . . . what about his future? Scholarships and all that?"

"Well, the boy's got to learn. There are consequences."

I look at the pictures on the wall behind him of former principals dating back to when this school first opened well over a hundred years ago. The pressure of their stares is too much for me. For Mr. Bains to sit there and tell me it's not my fault is like they're judging me, but punishing Tom.

"Try not to think of this as personal, but because of what happened, we're going to need to hold someone accountable."

But Tom? I was there, too. Worse, it was my idea. Yet I am the one who walked away unscathed. And now I'm also walking away without blame?

"For your sake and for the sake of the reputation of the school, I'm asking you to take a few days to formulate your statement. Get your dad to help you."

I leave the office, slinking through the halls, hoping not to be seen by anyone.

Mr. Kim follows me and says, "Hey, look on the bright side. You have a powerful family and a whole library named after you guys. You'll figure it out." I can't meet his eyes.

Mom's gabbing on the phone with her bestie when I get home. They're laughing over something. She must've heard the door because she comes out into the foyer.

"What are you doing home?" she mouths with her hand over the receiver.

"Long story," I say, slumping down on the plush white couch in the living room. I toss my backpack down on the floor.

"I have to go," Mom says to her friend and hangs up. "What's up?"

"Sit down."

All the colour goes from her face as I tell her about Tom being in the hospital. I want so badly to be able to stop there. It's enough.

"There's more," I say. I tell her about Yasmin, and she starts to shake her head and say "No. No. No." Over and over.

She looks at me as though I killed Yasmin myself. She looks at me the way she would look at a monster in a horror movie. I knew she'd look at me like that. That's why I couldn't say anything.

There. It's all out of me now. She sits in

front of me. There's nearly no expression on her face at all. It's like the time we almost hit a deer on the highway a few years back. The deer just stood there, stunned. Expressionless. That's what shock looks like.

We sit across from each other in silence for a really long time as I watch her try to come up with words other than *no*.

"We should call the doctor," she finally says.

"Why?"

"Maybe you have something. A fracture. Concussion. I don't know."

She whips out her phone and scrolls down to the hospital number. She explains the situation to the person on the other end. There's a pause and then, "Seriously? With all the money we donated, you expect us to wait two hours? Get over here. Now."

"I don't think there's any need," I say. I'm not the one who's hurt.

"I'm the parent. I'll say what's happening."

"Okay."

While we wait, I tell Mom about the upcoming funeral. She shakes her head and repeats the word *Saturday*.

"Yasmin Alvarez. Is she the one who dresses like a guy?"

"No, she's the one who wears those hippie scarves you hate." I pause. "Wore."

"I don't know who she is. I don't remember what she looks like. This is awful."

"You met her when you picked me up from yearbook club last year. She was the one who was eating a chocolate bar outside, and you told her she'd get fat if she kept that up."

"Oh, her. She was pretty."

"Yeah," I say. And for a moment it strikes me as weird that I never noticed until Whistler.

"Marcus, you're going to have to tell your dad tonight, and I'm not breaking the fall for you. Not this time. You're on your own with him."

"I know."

The only thing worse than telling my mom will be telling my dad.

Chapter 12

Dust and Ashes

After poking and prodding and getting every detail of the ski trip, Dr. Allen sits down on our living room chair.

"Looks like everything's fine," he says. "No fractures, nothing serious."

Nothing is fine, but I can't tell him that. Instead, I nod.

"You're lucky," he tells me.

"Lucky?"

"Think of your friends."

That's all I've been doing and all I can imagine doing. There's a movie playing in my mind, an endless loop of Yasmin's face, especially when her eyes lit up about skiing. There are flashbacks to jumps Tom took at the skateboarding park years ago, summers we ripped down the Baden-Powell trail, moments that are forever lost. As soon as Dr. Allen is out the door, my mom turns all neurotic again.

"We have to call the tailor. There's so much to do. You need a suit."

"Quit planning outfits, Mom."

She texts her friends or store owners or fashion designers or whatever.

"We've got a couple of errands to do," she says.

"Errands?" What could she possibly need? Milk? Eggs?

"I want your opinion. Come with me."

"About what?"

"Shoes for the funeral."

"Are you serious? That's what you

care about? Yasmin's dead and Tom's in a wheelchair, and you're buying shoes?"

"We have to look nice for the Alvarezes. They'd do the same for us." She looks dead serious.

"I can't believe you. This isn't some sort of social occasion. It's a funeral."

"You're getting a black suit made. That's final."

"I've already got one." My eyes fix on the chandelier above us. I don't want to go out. No way.

"That's your confirmation suit. You can't wear that." She raises her voice.

"It'll be fine."

There's that word again. But nothing is fine. I want to yell it at the top of my lungs. And no amount of shopping or getting stuff made will make it better. But my mom does not understand that.

That night, Mom hands me the phone. Dad's in Calgary overseeing some kind of development project. This is the last thing he needs. Every family issue is always the last thing he needs. That's the unspoken rule of our family.

"Stan here," he says.

"Hey, Dad. How's it going?"

"Busy. You?"

"Not so good."

I rattle off the events. It has become a sort of set story by now, a speech I've memorized. That makes me sad, that I've learned to tell the sequence of events.

"What?" he yells even though he has obviously heard me. He's shouting. "You were at our condo? Tell me it wasn't your idea. The Lees will want a settlement. How much is this going to cost me?"

"No, Dad. It's not like that."

"How do you know?"

"Well, Ed said it was an accident."

"He said that? Yeah, right. This'll call for a cheque, and a hefty one."

I can't believe this is what he's worried about. It's as though he has not even heard that Yasmin died.

"It's not like that," I say again.

"Like hell it's not. Do you know what happens when people get bills they can't pay? Oh, of course you don't." He scoffs.

That's a common dig. Whenever he's mad, my dad always launches into a lecture about how I don't understand anything and I won't until I'm older and less idealistic. Blah blah blah. He always makes it seem like nothing I have experienced can even come close to being hard, and for once, I just can't hear it.

"Dad!" I shout back. "Don't you understand? Tom will never walk again and Yasmin is dead."

Immediately after the words come out, I feel hot tears on my cheeks. I know if he were here, he'd have to fight really hard not to slap me across the face. But he isn't here. He's never here.

"What's the one rule I have for you, Marcus? The only frickin' rule I've ever told you to follow."

"Don't make a mess unless you have a powerful cleanup crew."

"That's right. How powerful is your crew? I tell you, this is the last time I'm fixing things for you. Once you're at Trinity, it's time to start greasing wheels yourself."

I hang up on him. It's the only time I've ever done it. I picture him huffing on the other end of the line, but it doesn't matter. Whatever he decides to do, say or worry about means nothing to me right now. All that matters is what I said to him. Tom will never walk again, and Yasmin is gone forever.

On Saturday morning, Mom is up with her hair in hot rollers. She has a mud mask on, which means she wants to look her best.

"Marcus, honey, eat something."

"My stomach's kinda not up to it," I say. It feels like I've just gotten off a roller-coaster ride and I'm about to lose my lunch, even though I have not eaten anything like a lunch for days. There's something about being full that seems wrong to me. I don't mind hunger pangs. In fact, hunger seems to suit me.

Pulling up to the church is surreal. I see a bunch of people from school and they feel like strangers somehow. The weirdest part is not having Tom there. Tom and I have always gone through everything together. I think about him lying in that hospital bed and it makes me want to retch.

When I finally gather the nerve to leave the car, I see a crowd of grade tens smiling and pointing at me and whispering. I don't even know their names. Clearly, they know mine.

Entering the church, the same thing happens. There are looks, pointing and a general hush as soon as I pass by. A couple of girls come up to me, asking if I'm okay. It's like they just want to get close to the action or something. Now I know what it's like to be a Kardashian at a red carpet event.

My mom is strangely at her best. All those years of going to business functions with my dad must have trained her to smile and nod and make it seem as though there's nothing weird about the fact that she and I are surrounded by curious guests who want to know what Yasmin's last words were.

Riaz is there. He shoots me a look like he wants to kill me. I wonder what the odds are of getting beat up in a church while sitting next to my mom.

The service starts and I bow my head and cry into my palms. I really don't know how people see me after that because I cannot look at them.

I am curious if any of them feel as broken as I do. If my mom hadn't made me, I doubt I'd even have been able to get out of bed. My body has been so heavy lately, as though gravity has a stronger pull than usual, but I think it's my heart that's the anchor.

The priest, or whatever that guy is called, talks about Yasmin's different backgrounds and how she grew up knowing God through several channels. It makes me think about that time she told me she was so over it. Then it makes me think about her telling me she was sick of being a good girl. I think about what happened in the elevator and how I could have done things differently.

I glance up at the front and see her face smiling back at me, at the whole room. I don't understand why her parents opted to use her school photo. It doesn't look like her. It doesn't capture her spirit at all. I am grateful I caught a glimpse of her at Whistler, and part of what's so sad is that I wish I had known her better. I keep wanting to correct the priest guy. He's talking in this really formal way and I want to burst out that he doesn't get her.

But then, I think this is probably how Yasmin would have wanted it. Her funeral is for her parents and her sisters. She did so much for them, so why not this, too? Listening to the sermon about all the times Yasmin took care of her sister, I am haunted by her comment that my life is easy and how good it must be to be me. All of that has turned into nothing but dust.

Chapter 13

Numb

When it's all over, people stand around shaking hands and greeting each other. Everyone in the seats in front of us and behind offer me their condolences as though I'm the one who suffered a major loss. Then Riaz glares from across the room. His posse joins him in staring me down. Mom is clever enough to dodge the crowd by pretending someone waved to her from afar. She ushers me out of there.

In the car, I say, "Thanks."

"Marcus, they're upset. They don't know who else to blame."

"I deserve it."

"You didn't push her over the cliff yourself."

"I practically did. I mean, not literally. The whole thing was my idea."

"No, honey. Don't say that," she whispers softly like she's soothing me after a scraped knee. "It's very brave of you to come today."

I shrug.

After she parks her Mini in the driveway and we're safe inside our big museum-like house, she locks the front doors and goes straight for the long white couch and flops herself down. She pries her Louboutin heels off using only her toes. The high-lacquer shoes with the red soles clunk on the carpet next to her.

"What a bunch of vultures." She places a decorative pillow over her face.

I sit down next to her on the matching sectional.

"Just be glad your dad wasn't there. He would not have known how to deal with that."

"The funeral?"

"The looks."

"But Yasmin is dead."

"You didn't kill her. Stop hinting you did. You'll only make things worse."

"But she's gone."

And she wouldn't be if not for me. All my mom cares about is her reputation.

"I need a glass of chardonnay," Mom says. That's my mom's answer to days like this, and I understand it. I'd numb out, too, if I could. Soon she'll get into her yoga pants, wipe off her makeup and call her bestie in Montreal to dissect this until she's slurring her words.

"You're still my little Marcus," she says.

It's awful that she can still love me after all this. I guess even the worst people on the planet are still loved by their mothers. I know I am supposed to be comforted by it, but instead it makes me question what kind of person she is. A killer-lover. A friend-hurter-lover. In the kitchen I grab a long-stemmed glass from the top shelf and one of the chilled bottles from the fridge. I place both items on coasters in front of her on the designer coffee table she loves so much. She doesn't even look my way.

"Thanks, hon." It comes out muffled from beneath the pillow.

All my life, my mom has enjoyed this image of us as the perfect family. To the outside world, my dad is successful, my mom's still good-looking and my sister, Steph, is smart. And I am my mom's very own little mascot that she can parade around to anyone who'll pay attention. Now that's over, and she has to see me for what I really am.

"I'm going to visit Tom," I say.

No answer.

I find my way to Tom's new room in a whole other ward of the hospital. The nurses all greet me with the kinds of smiles I am used to getting. They don't know I'm the scum of the earth.

Tom looks up when I walk in. He doesn't say hi. He looks back down.

"Hey, man," I say.

Again, silence.

"I said *hey*. Thought you'd want to hear about the funeral."

"Not from you."

"Tom."

"This is so messed up."

"I know." That's exactly what I've been trying to tell my mom.

Tom's holding his phone. I think he's playing some kind of video game, like I would have been. How else do you pass the time in a place like this? But I glance over and see he's on Yasmin's profile page.

The last update to her profile is a cartoon

picture of a slice of cake.

I look closer. It was posted at 12:37 a.m. on the night of the elevator.

Oh, shit.

"Dude, I, uh . . ."

In an instant, I'm transported back to the lobby and the elevator. In spite of the seriousness, I grin. I can't help it. She said she'd find a way to let us know that she shed the good girl stuff, but I didn't think she'd literally post about it.

Tom stares me down. "So it's true. You guys hooked up."

"I mean . . ." I put my hands in my pockets and fixate on the antique TV that's suspended from the ceiling. It's this boxy old thing.

"You know what? Whatever you have to say for yourself, I don't want to hear it. Screw you."

Her parents said at the funeral they were going to make her profile public so people could leave condolence messages there. I hadn't even looked yet. "I didn't know that was there."

Why am I saying this? Does it even matter? Tom glares, and then goes back to scrolling through Yasmin's pictures. I whip out my phone and do the same.

Most girls have tons of group pictures of people who look like they're having the best time ever. Yasmin has a bunch of photos of graffiti. There are all these close-up pictures of writing on mailboxes and concrete walls that say things like "love is all you need" and "there is beauty all around you."

Not sure what comes over me, I grab Tom's phone from him and turn it off.

"What the hell," he protests.

I put it down on the table next to him.

"That's not helping," I tell him. "It's not bringing her back."

"Don't tell me what to do. I'm so done with you telling me what to do."

"How long have you been staring at those pictures?"

After an awkward length of silence, Tom says, "I've got nothing to say to you."

I just stand there, feeling like a loser for a while before I finally say, "I'm gonna go."

He doesn't say anything as I walk out.

When I get home, my mom is through the first bottle of chardonnay. I can tell because the scene looks exactly like before but with an empty bottle in front of her. I go up to my room and get into my pyjamas. I brush my teeth without looking at myself in the mirror and then I get into bed.

I scan my social media and e-mail accounts, and there are a few notes from some of the girls at school. One feels bad and wants to hang out. The other says she's sad and wants to see me. I don't understand them. I wouldn't want to have anything to do with me. If I could avoid myself, I would.

I put on some music and stare at the

ceiling for a while. For the first time since I took it, I look at the selfie I got of the three of us right before everything went wrong. Yasmin's eyes look tired. I pull up her profile again on my phone and scroll through her photos. We hadn't friended before, and I didn't really know anything about her. Now I see that her parents have added pictures from when Yasmin was a kid. She was cute and goofy. So far, there are dozens of condolence messages. I want to write one, too, but it doesn't seem like the right thing to do.

I open a different window and reread the text message she sent me. I should delete it. Seems weird to have it. If she were still here, if everything were normal again, I'd look at this text with pride. I probably should delete it, but I don't.

Mom opens my door, so I turn away and hide my face in the pillow.

"Can't you knock?"

"I want you to see Dr. Allen again. We'll

get you some pills. A round of Paxil will make a world of difference."

"That's your answer to everything, isn't it?" I yell. I can't believe she can barge into my room like this and throw drugs at me. She did this back in grade nine, too, and it screwed me up for well over a year. It was more convenient for her, sure, but it was hell.

"You're in a state. It's chemical. You can fix it."

"Oh, yeah? You want me to numb out the way you do?"

"Marcus," she says in a soft voice. "I feel like I don't know you anymore."

I shrug. "Maybe you never did."

I don't know why I say that. It's mean. I'm mad because I don't believe that what I'm going through can be erased or made better by taking pills.

Besides that, Paxil makes it nearly impossible for me to get hard. My whole routine's been off anyway, since the accident. I was doing pretty well for awhile there with my daily tug in the shower. But since everything with Yasmin happened, I can't think of her that way, and when I think of anything that way, I think of her. And then I'm stuck. Throw Paxil into this mix, and I might as well get castrated. And Tom was the one worried that his equipment wouldn't work. It's almost funny.

* * *

At school, the stares are worse than at the funeral, and this time neither God nor my mom is there to ward off all the attention. I'm not sure what's worse, the groupies who want to talk to me about my feelings like I'm the victim in this whole mess or the guys who blame me. One thing's for sure. I've never been more popular in the hallways, and that in itself is depressing.

I am by my locker when Riaz walks by and slams into me. It's supposed to look like an accident, I'm sure, but it's obviously on purpose. He knocks the wind right out of me, and even though I'm not a small guy, he sends my body flying up against the metal lockers, making a clanging sound that causes everyone to turn and stare. Then he says, "Ooops."

He says nothing more after that.

As soon as he's out of earshot through the doors down the hall, his gang in tow, the anger inside me grows. It's as though a seed sprouted deep in my belly when all this went down and now it's growing out through my chest. Who is he to hit me? In spite of what his group thinks, I am not actually a murderer. He's the jerk who broke up with her and made her lose her mind. If anyone's at fault here, it's him. Without him being a royal class a-hole, she would not have been hanging out with Tom and me that night. There would have been no plan. She would be alive.

In that moment, all the rage I've ever known comes through as I punch the locker beside me. I hit it so hard my knuckles actually bleed, and I don't care. I welcome the pain. I want more of it. The physical sensation is better than the feeling that's been building up inside me. I cannot deal with that feeling. Blood is nothing compared to the wrath in me. Even if I break a few bones, who gives a crap?

It doesn't matter.

Chapter 14

Work

That afternoon, I get a text from Tom's dad.

Hey, Marcus. Ed here. Can you come by the house this afternoon? I need your help.

I text back.

No sweat. C u at 4.

He returns a smiley face.

After school, I drive past my street to the lower end of the canyon where Tom's family lives. The house looks different somehow, maybe because I am not here to visit Tom. There's a dark emptiness about it all.

Tom's Poh Poh comes to the door. Normally she greets me with kindness, but this time, she only holds the door and motions for me to go through the hall and kitchen.

"Ed out back," she says.

I walk through their house and she follows me to the kitchen. It was usually impossible to be in the kitchen with Poh Poh without her offering food. But today there's nothing.

The back door leads to a small yard and the garage we built, which is filled with Ed's tools and random supplies. Behind all that, hunched over the trunk of his car, is Ed. When he sees me, he smiles. I almost start crying at the first genuine smile I've seen since everything happened. Tom would be mad at his father if he could see his expression.

"Hey," I say.

"Hey."

"So, what do you need help with?"

"Well, I need to install this ramp here, and then some rails in the bathroom on the main floor. I don't know what to do with the stairs out front yet, but first things first."

"My dad can get a whole construction crew here in less than an hour."

"Marcus, I don't want you to hire people for me. I asked for *your* help."

I want to tell him he can always count on me, but there's a lump in my throat.

"Aren't you afraid I'll mess up like I did when we grouted the shower in the basement?"

"No, I'm not afraid of that. You'll be fine. We'll work together."

We haul the rails up from the garage through the kitchen to where Poh Poh is peeling yams while spying on us. Tom has always hated how she does that, eavesdrops on everything in the house, but I find it kind of comforting. It's different from my house where my mom just drinks and yaks with her friends, and my sister either isn't home or is locked in her room. And my dad's always on business.

The weird part is Tom not being there and knowing that he'd be totally pissed off if he knew that I was. As Ed and I work together on the first ramp installation, I get why he asked me. It's not that he needed someone to do this with him. It's that he needed *me*.

"So, listen," he says while making a pencil mark on the wall, "you can tell your dad I'm not signing the papers."

"What papers?"

"From the lawyers. The ones that say you're in no way at fault for Tom's injury."

"Are you kidding me? My dad sent you that?"

"They were dropped off yesterday. His suits showed up in person, no less."

My blood boils. "I can't believe my dad didn't even say anything to me about it."

"I'm not surprised. And I get why he sent them. He doesn't want to be liable."

"How's *he* liable?"

"Insurance lawyers are miracle workers. He doesn't want to get sued. You can go ahead and tell him I plan to take care of my family my own way. The part I object to is putting you in the free and clear. You can't just walk away from stuff like this, you know."

"Who's walking? I'm here, aren't I?"

"Yeah, you are. And that says a lot about you."

We continue working in silence. I help Ed haul more heavy equipment from the garage and he lets me use the drill. Later, when I drive away, I'm baffled that Ed has faith in me when my own father doesn't.

When I get home, Dad's lounging in the living room in his housecoat with his laptop out in front of him and a glass of red wine on a coaster next to him.

"You're home," he says when he sees me.

"*You're* home," I say. "When'd you get here?"

"I'm going to telecommute for a couple of days. The team can do without me, but I'm not sure you and your mom can."

I don't say that we've been managing just fine. Truth is, I'm not sure Mom has. She's taken a lot more time at the spa than usual and she's on the phone all the time. Maybe she's calling psychics or something.

I am so used to seeing Dad on Skype in his suit and tie that I'd almost forgotten the way he smells like Christian Dior cologne. I sit down on the couch opposite him.

"So, school got out a few hours ago. Where were you?"

"Helping Ed."

"Why? You know, the more you do that kind of thing, the more you look guilty."

"That's not true. Besides, he asked."

"What did he need help with?"

I tell him about the ramps and rails and other renovations that need to happen.

"So, you're his handyman?" There's a hint of disgust in his voice.

"No," I protest. "It's not like that. But that stuff *is* heavy."

What does my dad know about stuff like that? He's never done a day of labour in his life. He's the guy who pays others to work. He makes calls and signs contracts. He doesn't work himself, not with his hands, anyway.

"Did he say anything else?"

"Yeah, he said he's not signing your papers."

"I knew it. You just wait. Once he feels that squeeze, we're getting served. I'm telling you. That's human nature."

I hate that the way my dad sees Ed is so off base. What bugs me most is that my dad jumps to all these conclusions yet he's never spent any time with Ed. I don't even bother telling my dad what Ed told me. He wouldn't understand.

I've known Ed from sitting around at campfires, listening to stories about the first girl he kissed and what it was like to live on the beach in New Zealand that summer when he was eighteen. Ed taught me how to grout tiles and paint trim. Ed took my first fish off the line and helped me club it. He gutted it for me and showed me how to fillet it. We fried it up in butter and ate it with some Johnny's Seasoning Salt. Then we had roasted marshmallows. That's Ed. He isn't some lawsuit-slapping greedy jerk. He isn't like my dad.

He's like Tom. Or, really, Tom is like him. That's why I have to make things good between us again.

Chapter 15

Arrogance

After school, I swing by the hospital. It's been a few weeks since Tom told me to eff off and maybe he's cooled down since then. Even if he's still mad at me, I figure he'll be excited to have a visitor.

When I see him in his bed, I think I am looking at someone else. The guy in front of me seems like someone who's been through a war or something. He looks tough. He seems old and hardened by life.

"Tom?"

"What's up?" He asks in a tone that isn't light-hearted and friendly, but calculating, like he's part of a gang and sizing me up.

"Not much . . . I've been helping your dad out with some construction around the house."

"I heard."

"He asked. What was I supposed to do?"

He doesn't answer right away. Just sits there for a while first. "You know what's sad and pathetic? I used to want to be like you. Ever since we met, I always wanted the stuff you had, the better equipment, the cooler mountain bike and that weird magnetism you have that gets you girls. I could say it's the trust fund, but I don't think it's just the money. It's the confidence and security that it gives you. I wanted all that, but you know what I realized? If I had that, I'd have to be you, and I would hate to be you."

"Tom . . ."

"Save it. The last thing I need is for you

to waltz into this whole situation and turn yourself into some kind of hero just because you picked up a hammer. I don't want to be wheeled into the gym at the end of the year to watch you receive some kind of community service award for helping me."

His face is red, his voice low and serious. If he could punch me from where he is, he would, but his words hurt more.

"I guess you want me to go."

"Yeah."

I stand there, not believing him. Is this really how it ends? Just like that? Four years of friendship and spending all our free time together comes to a crashing halt. I look down at my sneakers, willing my feet to move me, but they won't. I can't leave him lying there.

"Who else has visited you?" I ask.

"Not your business, but I'll have you know, I've got plenty of friends. I don't need you."

He's so sure of himself and he's convinced

that I am the enemy. Friends don't look at each other the way he's looking at me, with the eyes of a hawk about to swoop down and eat a mouse.

"Well, uh, okay, see ya." It's a stupid thing to say, but I don't know what words are right. I don't go, though. I just stand there.

"You know, your dad tried to give my family fifty grand in exchange for a signature that says you didn't do anything wrong."

"What's so wrong with that? You guys need the money. Is it not enough?"

"It's not about money, Marcus. You're so friggin' dense sometimes."

"Isn't it, though? Your dad told me how much all these house alterations are going to cost. Obviously it matters a little bit."

He scoffs at me. "You know that scene in *A Tale of Two Cities* with the marquis and the coin?"

I shrug. "Come on, that was for English. You know I didn't read it."

"Actually, yeah, I do know because I gave you all the answers, but that's not my point. My point is that what your dad did was like that scene, and that's why my dad's pissed and me too."

Dammit. Who knew he'd talk in code? "What's it about?"

"It's about respect. Something your family obviously doesn't have."

"Wait. What happens in the scene?"

"Read it yourself if you give a crap." He pulls the hospital curtain cord to create a barrier between us. Conversation over. This time, there's nothing left for me to do but leave.

One of the nurses smiles at me on the way out. I can't even meet her eyes. I walk out of that wing of the hospital and take the elevator down to the main floor. Everything is in slow motion again. It's that same feeling I had right after the accident, like I am in quicksand.

There's no way I am going to be able to

drive, so I sit down on a bench in the middle of the lobby, like some kind of sad old person who just found out that the person they spent their life with has died.

* * *

When I get home, Mom's actually cooked. That's unheard of. I didn't even know she had it in her. When Dad's out of town, she eats salads or gets catered meals delivered. But tonight, she's made lasagna, my dad's favourite, and she sets the table really nicely, too.

Between bites, she says, "I think we should have the Alvarezes over when the dust has settled."

Yasmin's parents? Is she crazy?

"You guys don't even know each other," I argue.

"No, but still."

"Mom, that's crazy."

"I'm with Marcus this time," Dad says,

holding his glass of merlot. "If anything, we need to distance ourselves."

"I disagree. If we do that, he looks guilty. We need to think of the future of how this all plays out."

My mom, the strategist. No wonder she's on the books as Dad's PR consultant. She's all about public perception. And my dad's all about money and power.

I can't believe that I never noticed how shallow they are.

After dinner, I excuse myself and go to my room. I'm sure it suits them perfectly to be left to their own plans.

In my room, I try to watch a movie on TV but I can't concentrate. It's just some stupid comedy with Ashton Kutcher, but after about fifteen minutes, I realize I can't even follow the story. I have no idea who anyone is or what's happening.

Like a goldfish swimming from one side of its boring bowl to the other, I get up and wander over to my bookcase, opening the glass door for no real reason. That's when I spot the English novel.

I take *A Tale of Two Cities* off the shelf, but I can't bring myself to read it. It's heavy. Even rifling through the pages seems hard. Why did Dickens write so much? I put the book back. Online, I find the SparkNotes summary video. That's better. At first I kind of skip through, scanning for a coin — it's an eighteen minute video, after all — but then I start to watch it.

A badass cartoon villain comes through a poor town. His carriage runs over a boy and the boy survives, but he'll probably never walk again. Without skipping a beat, the villain takes out a gold coin and tosses it at the kid's dad. Then he just leaves like they're even. Like it's totally dealt with.

Oh, man.

Chapter 16

Nobody

I sit down on my bed. I have messed up
more than I even realized. It all starts to click
that everything I have learned is wrong. Like
in Economics, we learned this fancy word,
meritocracy. It means that if you work hard and
do the right stuff, you can have all the same
stuff as everyone else. It means there's a level
playing field out there. But that's a lie. That's
what Tom's been trying to tell me all along, but
I've been too stupid to understand it.

It's like I'm at the bottom of a well, but the bottom keeps sinking. Just when I think I've sunk as low as I can, I realize that I can go lower still.

Everything that happened is permanent. Even at my high school reunion, I'll still be the guy who put Tom Lee in a wheelchair. I'll still be the guy who sent Yasmin Alvarez hurtling to her death. I will be exactly what Yasmin and Tom said I was: a spoiled rich kid who only thinks about himself.

I go into Mom's bathroom and open her medicine cabinet. There's my dad's blood pressure medication and a ton of vitamins and supplements, mostly weight-loss stuff with skinny people in swimwear on the bottles. Tucked away behind all of that is Mom's dirty little secret. I don't think Dad knows about the Oxazepam. The bottle has about twenty pills left. I clench it in my fist and take it with me as I close the mirror door of the cabinet.

As I come out from the en suite into my

parents' bedroom, Mom comes in.

"What are you doing here?"

"Nothing," I say.

"Why not use your own bathroom, then?"
She gives me a grimace.

"I was looking for something."

"For what?"

Uh . . .

"Sunscreen," I say, improvising. That
makes no sense. But she buys it. She's drunk.

"Well, did you find it?"

She goes into their bathroom and pulls
out a drawer. I shove the bottle of pills into the
front pocket of my hoodie so that when she
hands me the tube of lotion, I am able to reach
for it, empty-palmed.

"Thanks."

"Yeah, sure."

She gives me a weird look like she knows I
didn't even open the drawer.

Back on my bed, I examine the bottle. It
says she's supposed to take only half a tablet

and only once in a while. *How strong is this stuff? Is this the way to go?* I stay flat on my bed for a long time, feeling the waves of pain come crashing over me. How badly I want this feeling to end. I don't want to exist anymore. I don't deserve to. Life handed me every advantage and what have I done?

But the thought of all that blackness, the empty void, scares me. I don't want to die. Not this way and not yet. At Yasmin's funeral, there was all this bullcrap talk about her being in a better place and being with God, and it makes me want to puke to think of it. She was full of life. She didn't want to die and she didn't mean to. There's no way to make it right. I lie there for a really long time until I feel Mom's pasta dinner rumbling around in my insides. No matter what I decide, I need to get rid of this ache first.

In my bathroom, I sit down on the toilet hoping to relieve myself of the cramp in my gut. On the counter, there's a razor. It's not like I mean for my gaze to land on it. It just happens. Then I can't unsee it. I have some unused ones in the cupboard beneath. If you believe in signs from the universe and all that crap, then there are definitely objects in front of me that remind me how quickly and easily I could end it all.

I have everything I need, except for one thing. Courage.

* * *

The next day, in homeroom, Ozzie says, "What's it like now that you don't have Tom following you around anymore?" He's being his regular old idiotic self, trying to get in on whatever action is going on, I guess.

"So you do know his real name," I say. I want to punch him.

"Don't be so touchy," he snaps. "He'll get better and follow you around again in no time. You'll see."

I roll my eyes at him. What do you even

say to a guy like that?

Kayla comes over to sit next to me and says, "Maybe everyone will finally stop calling him Worm."

"Yeah, maybe . . ."

"How did he get that name, anyway?" she asks, probably trying to wipe her hands clean of the fact that she's the one who gave him the name in the first place.

"Because people are morons." I say it loud enough that Ozzie can hear.

Between classes, I get stopped in the hall when this Socials teacher I don't even know comes out of his classroom. "Marcus?"

"Yeah."

"I heard about Tom and I'm sorry."

"Thanks," I say.

"Tell him Mr. D wants him to get better soon, okay?"

"Yeah, sure."

I feel like I have some kind of grief sign on me. I'm not Tom's only friend, am I? Why does everyone keep talking as if I am?

I go to the washroom to take a quick leak before heading back to my locker, and that's when I see red-eyed Riaz, washing his face in the sink. It's obvious he's been crying.

"Go. Just go," he says, pointing toward the door.

I turn to leave.

"Wait a sec," he says before I even take a step. "I don't want to ask, but I have to know. What was the last thing she said?"

In that moment, I decide to edit. Looking at him, so desperate to make sense of something that will never be right, I figure there's a whole lot he doesn't need to know.

"She said you were a good guy."

"She said that?" he asks. He shoos me away with a single gesture, but I see the tears stream down his cheeks even before I turn around.

After school, I drive home. Dad has left again to take care of business, as he puts it. I am glad he's gone.

In the living room, Mom is in a downward dog position being told to love herself from a DVD. I go the other way, into the kitchen, and throw a frozen dinner into the microwave without even checking what kind it is.

There's a hum as the little plastic rectangle goes around and around. Tom's words come at me again, and I think about the marquis and the injured boy and Tom's glare.

Gross food comes out piping hot. I put it on plate and take it upstairs to my room even though Mom hates when I do that. I don't want to overhear any more of her feel-good garbage.

I shovel the disgusting pasta into my mouth only because I have to eat. I am glad I'm not enjoying it. It seems wrong to enjoy anything ever again. On my laptop, I look at Yasmin's page. I don't know if I want to feel close to her or Tom. Maybe I just want that night back, the night it was all perfect and unbroken. I wish we'd taken a photo of that night. I can't stand to look at the selfie of us on the mountain.

I was such a jerk that weekend. Tom has every reason to hate me. I think about the kind of a-hole I was becoming before that weekend. Here I was, likely headed for Trinity College with all kinds of awards for extra-curricular community service. *Ha.* My parents were ready to fork over the money for it. Four years later, I'd come back from Ontario with a slick degree and lots of powerful contacts, and my dad would offer me the family business. Through really no effort of my own, except following instructions, I would become the head of an already sizable empire.

When Yasmin told me life was easy for me, I didn't know what she meant. I get it now. I'm the most spoiled guy I know.

But there's more to the story than she knew. What she didn't realize is that my life looks awesome on the surface, but really I've always been my dad's puppet and my dad will always be the kind of man who is on the alert that the Ed Lees of the world are out to sue him. The saddest thing of all is that in all these years, the only person who accepted me, a-hole that I was, was Tom. Tom never cared what my parents did. He has never given a crap about status and brands and reputation. All along, he's been there for dirt biking, skateboarding, surfing, camping and fishing. We've done all these awesome things together, and I tried to take his girl, put him in a wheelchair and killed Yasmin. And to top it all off, I saw nothing wrong with my dad just throwing money at the problem like he always does. And, yeah, I did kind of think it was good of me to help Ed with the rails, like that's even anything at all.

I guess Tom finally sees me for who I really am. A real nobody.

Chapter 17

Hard Reset

I come home the next day to find that Mom has left a big thick envelope from Trinity College, University of Toronto, on my bed. When I open it, it says they're pleased to have me in their International Relations program. I got residence in a building that looks like a castle. I got a place among the kids of the rich and powerful. Everything's fantastic. I toss the whole shebang into the recycling bin under my desk and face-plant on my mattress.

The thing is, it doesn't matter what kind of degree I get or where I get it from, what awards I win, what kind of contacts I have or how much money I make. My future is always going to include this part of me and I hate that. I don't have a future at all.

I spent the night sitting at my desk and thinking about everything I've lost and how quickly it all happened. It was a snap of the finger, a moment I wish I could erase from history, but that's impossible. I haven't had an ounce of alcohol since the night before everything turned horribly wrong and I probably won't drink again. *How can I?*

I've tried to get back my morning ritual of jerking off in the shower, but it's pointless. I can't do it. All I think about is Yasmin, how she made me feel good and how she's gone. So that part of my life is done. I might as well become a monk or something.

I can't get on my bike without thinking about Tom. I'll obviously never ski again.

There's so much that's over for good.

I e-mail Trinity and tell them thanks anyway, but I'm not coming.

✻ ✻ ✻

Not two days pass before I get a call.

"What the hell are you thinking?" Dad's voice shouts at me. "You turned down Trinity? Do you have any idea what kinds of favours I had to do to get you a spot?"

My dad. Forever wheeling and dealing.

"There's been a change of plan," I say. I want to add "which you would know if you lived here," but I don't say anything. It isn't his fault I am so messed up.

"Like hell there has. Everything I did in my life was for you. You know that?"

Here we go.

"I know, Dad." I know everything he's about to say.

"I got you every kind of tutor, every kind

of equipment, membership, private school. You got it all, Marcus. Do you know most kids would give their right arm for the kinds of things you got? Your friend Tom would have. Believe me. And the thanks I get is *what*? You decide you're not going? What's your plan, then? Sit at home and be depressed? Live off your trust fund?"

"No. I dunno."

"Do you know what would have happened if I had just stayed home every time I felt depressed? I'll tell you what. Mediocrity. Is that what you want? You want to be mediocre?"

As if I wouldn't trade all of the family wealth to have had him attend even just one softball game instead of getting hammered with clients and VIPs. As if I wouldn't give it all up to have gone fishing with him instead of with Tom and Ed.

"Dad, I . . ." *Oh, man, it's like slapping the guy right across the face.* "I made up my mind. I'm gonna go volunteer. Build some houses. Do something useful for a change."

Silence. I imagine him going over my words carefully in his mind while he sips his wine. Then there's the click of a lighter. *Oh, great.* I'm now also the reason Dad's smoking again. *Add it to my list of damages inflicted on humanity.*

"Marcus, Marcus." I can tell he's shaking his head at me and I am glad I can't see it. "It's not your fault, you know. You all made choices that day, stupid choices. But choices. Yasmin didn't have to go with you. You didn't force Tom to do what he did. And his accident doesn't have to cost you your future."

"That's not it, Dad."

I can't tell him I don't want to be like him, living for status symbols and a glass of Shiraz at four o'clock in the afternoon.

"I probably should have taken you to more construction sites when you were younger. I protected you too much."

I need to prove myself, but I can't even

talk to him about it because he's done it. He inherited an empire and made it grow. What have I done? Not a damn thing. It's weird. If I go get myself a government job or something normal that pays whatever normal people get paid, it won't be good enough for him. It'll never be good enough.

Thinking about that makes me sad, so I tell my dad I have to go.

* * *

I walk into the rehab centre, and in the foyer there are a few people my age sitting around chatting in their wheelchairs. They look at me and stop talking. My heart pounds. This is not my world and I don't feel welcome. I haven't talked to Tom for a few weeks, since he was transferred from Lions Gate, and something tells me he doesn't want me to come.

But you know how it is. Sometimes it doesn't matter what other people want. You have to do what you have to do and I have to see Tom.

Ed gave me a room number, but I still need a directory to figure out what floor to go to.

A middle-aged woman in a four-wheeler scooter is doing some kind of needlepoint or knitting by the bulletin board. She has on a rainbow tie-dyed muumuu, and when she sees me, she looks up from her craft.

"What are you looking for?" she asks.

"It's okay," I say. "I'll figure it out."

"I know this place like the back of my hand. Let me help you." She takes the piece of paper Ed gave me and looks at it. "Oh, you have to take the elevator down a floor to the youth wing."

"Thanks," I say. It's usually such a pain when older people want to help you, but she's kind of cool in her own way.

I get out of the elevator and there are all kinds of posters and bright cheerful colours, but the florescent lights and the clinical chemical smell make it feel hospital-like anyway.

I turn the corner and peer into the room Tom's in. He has his back to the door and he is sitting with some other guy. They're joking around. My stomach's in knots. I don't belong here and I want to go.

The guy looks at me. "Can I help you with anything?"

"Oh, uh . . ."

Tom turns around. "Hey, man."

"Hey," I say, at ease because he's at least making eye contact with me, not giving me the hateful death stare anymore.

"What's up?" Tom asks.

"Not much with me. I came to see what's new with you."

"I'll give you two some time," the guy says. I thought he was paralyzed, too, but he gets up out of the wheelchair he was sitting in and pushes it out in front of him.

"I'll let you take this one for a spin later," he says to Tom. They fist-bump each other like the guy is some kind of camp counsellor or something.

After he's gone, I ask, "So what's that all about?"

"Oh. Nothing," Tom says. "Chair envy."

"Huh?"

"Yeah, this new guy came into the centre and he got injured at school, so he got all kinds of funding, and that thing right there is like the Rolls Royce of chairs and Dan said I could try it out later. That's all."

"Oh," I say. Why is it that wheelchairs give me pangs of anxiety? If I am going to stay friends with Tom, I have to be more chill. But it's still a weird thing for me to see him like this.

"Hey, you know, maybe it's not so bad, all this," I tell him as if to convince myself. It's a big *maybe*, but Tom always finds silver linings in places most people can't.

"Dude. I'm only going to say this once. Quit pitying me."

"I don't," I protest.

"Uh, yeah, you do." His voice is firm.

"That's not true," I insist.

"It's kind of true. I've known you way too long for you to be able to hide what you're thinking. You look at me and you think I'll never get a girlfriend. I'll have to get some kind of equity job. My life will suck from now on. There's no way around it. All the stuff I was working toward like university is all over. I can tell that's what you think about when you look at me."

"Wait a second. What? You're giving up on university?"

"I can't go."

"They have ramps."

"Yeah, well . . . I guess I'm just being whiny." His tone is sarcastic.

"Come on, Tom."

"Do you realize how much it costs to be in

a wheelchair? My dad had to put in an elevator to get me up the stairs. There's no way I'm asking for even just a tiny bit of tuition money. It's all on me now. And you know Bains — I'm not eligible for any scholarship anymore, and I'll have to try to explain my expulsion. All those old dreams are over."

"You can still follow your dreams," I say like I need to be the positive one. It sounds like the bullshit on Mom's workout videos.

"Yeah. Well, you know what? Having all this time to think about my life has made me realize that I want to take a different direction. I'm not the guy I was before."

"Sure you are," I say and try to think of a joke to cheer him up. Something we always laughed at would do, but nothing comes to mind.

"You don't get it," he says and looks in the opposite direction. "I don't want to be that guy anymore. I'm glad I never have to go back to Montrose."

"I thought you liked school."

He shrugs. "I didn't like getting called Worm all the time."

"You didn't exactly fight it."

"Well, like I said, I've had a lot of time to think and I'm not that guy anymore. I've got stuff I want to do."

"Like what?"

"Been tinkering with a business idea."

"You have?" I can't hide my surprise. I think if I were stuck in a place like this, a pathetic little room in the basement of a rehab centre, I'd be all kinds of depressed. "What kind of business?"

"Outdoor tourism."

"You mean like bus tours?"

"Yeah, that. But also a ton of other stuff. You know how when you're on the ferry, there's like five million pamphlets you can pick up with cool things to do? I want to organize some of those cool things. You know how I feel about the outdoors."

I'm surprised to hear him say it since the outdoors was not so good to him last time, but I get it. You have to get back on the horse. At least, Tom does.

"What about getting your old job back at Mountain Equipment Co-op?"

"I might, short term. But in the long run, I don't want to work for someone else. I've got big plans."

It's so weird to see him looking almost, like, happy. How's he happy while I'm so messed up? For some reason, I think of that night with the pills and the razor, how they called me to them and cast a kind of spell over me, telling me to end it right then and there.

"Can I ask you something?"

"What?"

"All this time, I dunno. Did you ever . . . Did it ever cross your mind to . . . I dunno . . . end it?"

"You mean suicide?"

I nod.

"We talk a lot about it here. I mean, some people come up against some pretty dark stuff."

"What about you?" I ask. I don't want to hear about the other folks in here.

"I thought about it. Sure. I think everyone who gets a hard reset like this kind of wonders whether it's worth it to go on. But I could never do that to my family. I mean, I think about everything they've done for me and are still doing for me and I just . . . I could never."

"You're going to be fine, aren't you?" I ask. I don't mean for the question to come out sounding like I'm surprised, but it does.

"I have no choice, do I? I gotta be better than fine. I gotta rock out."

"Cool," I say. I want to tell him about my own thoughts, but for now, it doesn't matter. Maybe one day, when he's out of here, we can have a longer man-to-man.

"Yeah, chairs have come a long way and so has technology. You know, I can go boating, drive a bus, go hang-gliding, take people rock climbing. You name it, I can do it."

"Sounds like you've got this whole life in a wheelchair thing figured out," I say.

"Not totally, not yet, but eventually," he says. "Besides, chicks dig it."

"What?" I'm sure I've misheard him. "When do you have time for girls?"

He grins. "I've had more action in rehab than ever before in my life. There's this one girl who calls me Hot Wheels."

I laugh and shake my head. "You should go for it."

"Nah. I'm still hung up on Yasmin. That was two years of my life, man."

"I really didn't know she meant that much to you."

"I told you she did."

"I probably wasn't paying attention."

Amazingly, Tom laughs. And I do, too.

Chapter 18

Killer Fire

After that day, visiting Tom at the centre after school is my routine. Sometimes I bring him frozen yogurt, sometimes a burger. Whatever he texts that he wants, I bring it. Sometimes he doesn't want to see me at all, but I still come by.

Winter turns into spring. I help Ed at the house. June comes around. I graduate. Tom starts talking about online business programs that don't cost as much as university. He crunches numbers and rattles off business names. Sometimes I think he's going a bit bonkers in there, like a rat in a cage. Other times, I seriously envy him. I still have no clue what I'll be doing come September but I'm waiting to hear back from Habitat for Humanity, so that's something.

One early July day, Tom gets all serious and says, "I need to ask you to do something."

"Okay."

"So you know how I'll be going home in a few weeks?" he asks. "There's some stuff in my room I don't want."

"Okayyy . . ." I say, kind of confused. Why not deal with that later?

"Remember when I told you I'm glad I'm not the guy I used to be?"

"Yeah?"

"Well, like, I'm really glad."

"What are you getting at?"

"It's time to kill the Worm, man."

"Huh?"

"Me and some of the people here were talking the other night at our group meeting. We're going to have this big bonfire. Say goodbye to some stuff. Kill off the parts of us we don't need anymore."

"What stuff do you need?"

"My skateboard for one thing." He looks more determined than I've ever seen before. "The Worm dies Friday, and you're going to help me kill him. Get ready."

This gets to me. I'm past tears in all this, but it makes me sad anyway. The Worm was my best friend.

"That's cool," I say. "Make me a list."

* * *

Ed's out front, clipping the hedges back, when I pull into the driveway.

"I'm on a mission," I tell him.

"Oh, yeah?"

"Tom wants me to bring some of his old

stuff down to the rehab centre for a bonfire."

"A what?"

"It's a therapy thing." I don't want to tell Ed that we're killing off Worm.

"All right. Door's open."

He goes back to shearing the hedges around the old house. There's a lot that I want to tell him — that he's been a better dad to me than my own, that he's the guy who taught me to use a hammer, to use my hands and my heart. But it seems cheesy to say it.

Tom's room has an eerie feel to it. There's a musty scent like the door had been closed all this time, and I wonder what it has been like for his family to live with this kind of emptiness.

I get out Tom's gym bag and fill it with soccer cleats, basketball shoes and a baseball glove. There's the yearbook from grade ten that has a bunch of Worm references and a whole page that Ozzie drew a big long worm on. Tom'll probably want to at least rip the page out. His skateboard is stashed against the wall and I grab it, shoving it under my arm. I heave it all down the stairs and into the Jeep.

Killing off Worm is really getting to me. It's like I don't want to see him go because we have a lot of great memories, but I also understand that Tom needs to do this. Maybe I need to, too. The old Marcus isn't going anywhere, either. That guy's doomed. The more I think about what we went through together, the more I see that I have to do exactly what Tom is doing. Out with the old. Make room for the new.

On my way home, I pull over in front of the Toronto Dominion Bank and go in. The branch manager comes right up to me and shakes my hand.

"Hey, Marcus," he says. "What can I do you for?"

He laughs. I guess he thinks he's funny.

"I need a favour," I tell him.

"Sure thing."

Minutes later, he fobs us into a room upstairs. He produces a little key to my family's safety deposit box. I glance at my grandmother's diamonds, and for just a second, it makes me sad that such shiny jewels live in this dark little tomb.

I take what I need.

"Thanks, man," I tell the branch manager.

"Any time," he says. "Say hi to your dad."

Epilogue

Heading to the centre, I realize it has been exactly six months since our lives changed forever. I still wish I could go back in time and change everything. I still think about Yasmin several times a day. I still wonder if Tom can ever really forgive me.

A few of Tom's friends gather around the fire pit. All told, there are six of us and I am the only one who isn't in a chair. I build up the kindling first, like Ed taught me. It feels good to be able to make a fire for us, but I also don't want to rob anyone else of the chance to do it.

Tom has his gym bag full of memories on the ground beside him. The fire's blazing. I toss on a log and it takes.

"Later, skater," Tom says, chucking the skateboard first. It doesn't take long for the fire to catch. As it goes up in flames, I look over at Tom. His expression surprises me. He's beaming.

His face is warm in the glowing amber light of the fire. The heat ripples from the pit. Nobody says anything. It's enough to watch the green toxic fumes of the lacquered board turn into a smelly cloud of smoke. It's enough to sit quietly and remember all the times we'd skated around Ambleside, in the skate park and at school.

He tosses his basketball onto the fire, too. I don't understand why that one needs to go. We played wheelchair basketball back in grade eight gym class. It was insanely hard, but we did it, and I imagine Tom will do it again. Being athletic isn't over for him. In my mind's eye, I see him catching fish again, going camping and even hang-gliding, like he mentioned. It'll be different, but he'll figure out a way. Just like he'll figure out a way to get over Yasmin and have sex.

The other people there toss in the remnants of their old lives, too. There's this girl a few years younger than us who throws in her figure skates. And this man who's maybe in his mid-twenties, he tosses in a Frisbee and explains how this one isn't the actual Frisbee that he jumped for that day, but his injury was from jumping into a lake while playing Ultimate — right onto the rocks beneath the surface of the water.

After everyone has gone, I ask if I can throw something in, too. I open up my backpack and reach in for the part of myself that I want to kill off. I toss in my trust fund papers.

"Wait a second," Tom says. "Is that what I think it is? You're burning your whole financial future?"

I nod.

"Dude, what the hell!" Tom shouts as he figures out what I'm doing.

I shrug. "It has to be done. If I'm really going to be a man on my own terms, I can't keep them. I don't need them anymore."

"Wow." He sits in silence for a long time. "No matter what happens, I just want you to know you can always come work for me."

I punch him in the shoulder. He punches back.